LITTLE WOMEN

"Curls around your face would be very flattering," Amy suggested to Meg.

"I'll fix your hair for you," Jo volunteered. She wound paper around strands of Meg's hair and clamped the hot metal tongs tight.

"Are the curls supposed to smoke like that?" Beth asked.

"It's just the dampness drying," Jo said.

"What a smell!" Amy said. "Reminds me of burnt feathers."

"Just as soon as I take off these papers you'll see a cloud of little lovely ringlets," Jo promised. But when she unclamped the tongs, out came almost all of Meg's lovely bangs.

"Oh, what have you done? I'm bald!" Meg wailed. "I can't go to the party like this!"

Books by Laurie Lawlor

Addie Across the Prairie
Addie's Dakota Winter
How to Survive Third Grade
The Worm Club
Little Women *(a movie novelization)*

Available from MINSTREL Books

LITTLE WOMEN

A Novel by **Laurie Lawlor**
Based on the motion picture screenplay
by **Robin Swicord**
From the novel by **Louisa May Alcott**

A **MINSTREL**® **BOOK**

PUBLISHED BY POCKET BOOKS

New York   London   Toronto   Sydney   Tokyo   Singapore

A MINSTREL PAPERBACK *Original*

 A Minstrel Book published by
POCKET BOOKS, a division of Simon & Schuster Inc.
1230 Avenue of the Americas, New York, NY 10020

Copyright © 1994 by Columbia Pictures Industries, Inc.

Artwork copyright © 1994 by Columbia Pictures Industries, Inc.

ISBN: 0-671-51902-6

First Minstrel printing December 1994

10 9 8 7 6 5 4 3 2 1

A MINSTREL BOOK and colophon are registered trademarks of Simon & Schuster Inc.

Printed in the U.S.A.

One

~

No stars shone above Concord, Massachusetts, on Christmas Eve 1863. Bruised-looking gray clouds prowled the night sky. The air smelled of snow and wood smoke. Returning soldiers turned up the frayed collars of their blue coats and trudged through the muddy streets. Some hobbled into the bitter wind on crutches. Others paused wearily when blasts of fine, sharp flakes sent their empty sleeves twisting, turning. Bull Run. Antietam. Chancellorsville. Gettysburg. After three long years, would Mr. Lincoln's bloody war ever end?

Wind rattled dead vines that clung to the outside of a three-story brown clapboard house on the corner of Hawthorne and Lexington roads. A few holly branches tied with a piece of red flannel decorated the arched entrance. On first glance there seemed nothing unusual about the place. It was not so different from other weatherbeaten houses in Concord and certainly not as elegant as the stately stone mansion that stood next door. What made this house special was the muffled sound of laughter and the warm glow of light coming from an attic window, just below the eaves of the steep gabled roof.

Inside the attic, a club called the Pickwick Society was having its weekly secret meeting. Mr. Pickwick, Mr. Snodgrass, Mr. Tupman, and Mr. Winkle sat around a cluttered table surrounded by broken chairs, two leather trunks, a battered couch, a dusty bird cage, and a large tin box. None of the miniature gentlemen seemed to mind the mess. They were too busy sharing the latest issue of their newspaper, the *Pickwick Portfolio.*

Mr. Snodgrass adjusted the black top hat on his head and opened the large page of smudged newsprint. Boldly he tipped back in his chair, thrust his enormous boots onto the table, and nearly knocked over six candle stubs burning in six creamed corn cans.

"Do sit properly!" demanded Winkle, who sported a green oversize frock coat, a moth-eaten gray wool scarf, and a monocle. "You needn't show off your fancy boots and cause us all to be crisped in a terrible confabulation!"

Snodgrass snorted. "I think you mean *conflagration.*" He tossed one end of his long, elegant green cravat over his shoulder and plunked his wondrous feet back on the floor. Then he began to read in a loud melodious voice: " 'On Friday last, we were startled by a violent shock in our basement, followed by cries of distress. On rushing to the cellar, we discovered our beloved president prostrate upon the floor, having tripped and fallen while getting firewood—' "

"Stop!" interrupted Pickwick, the president of the society. He rapped his unlit pipe on the table. When he jumped to his feet, the cuffs of his enormous brown coat dropped below his dainty fingertips. "That accident never would have happened if we still had enough servants."

"I'm sorry you're embarrassed, but this is the most interesting news we have for this week," Snodgrass said, then continued, " 'A perfect scene of ruin met our eyes. Mr. Pickwick had plunged his head and shoulders into a tub of water, upset a keg of soft soap upon his manly form, and torn his garments badly.'"

Winkle chuckled. He stopped as soon as he noticed Pickwick's nasty glare.

"'On being removed from this perilous situation, it was discovered that he had suffered no injury but several bruises, and we are happy to add he is now doing well.'"

"Bravo! Bravo!" shouted Tupman and Winkle.

But Pickwick continued to pout.

"Oh, Meg, don't spoil everything!" Snodgrass cried impatiently. He slipped off his top hat. Down tumbled marvelous thick brown unruly hair, revealing that Mr. Snodgrass was not a gentleman at all. Mr. Snodgrass was a seventeen-year-old girl named Jo March, who had the long-legged, awkward grace of a chestnut colt. Like her three sisters—disguised as Tupman, Winkle, and Pickwick—Jo had dressed up in men's cast-off clothing for their weekly Pickwick Society meeting.

"Be a sport," Jo pleaded on one bent knee before eighteen-year-old Meg. "Readers love dramatic accidents."

"I'm glad I wasn't the one who fell into the tub," said twelve-year-old Amy. She had a habit of saying the first thing that came into her blond curly head. "What if I'd broken all the fingers in my right hand and could never draw again?" She sniffed and poked a finger through one of the holes in Winkle's gray wool scarf.

"Let's be thankful no one was seriously hurt," suggested fourteen-year-old Beth, wise beyond her years. She unpinned Tupman's paper badge, which said P.S., for Pickwick Society, and began mending a sock. "Now give us a smile, Meg dear."

Meg smiled wanly. Her skin was fair, her hair soft brown, and her eyes large and dark. Pretty Meg was the oldest and most sensitive of the March sisters and could not bear to be abused by anyone's jokes or stories, not even Jo's.

Amy sighed. "My favorite article is still 'The Masked Marriage.'"

"You ought to publish that story, Jo," Beth said, "and not just in the *Pickwick Portfolio.*"

Jo jumped up and bowed, pleased by the idea. She formally presented the smudged newsprint to Meg and kissed her on the top of her head. "Mr. Pickwick, I believe Mr. Tupman is insulting our fine newspaper."

The sisters laughed. Jo pulled the handle of a broken croquet mallet from a box and began to sword fight with her shadow.

"What I want to know, Jo," Beth said, "is how

you come up with something to write. I seldom think of any good ideas."

"I rather liked your piece, Tupman, 'The History of a Squash,' " Meg teased.

"The first rule of all writing, Mr. Tupman—never write what you know." Jo made a dramatic lunge and flipped her weapon behind the couch.

"I love forbidden marriages set in strange foreign places," Amy declared. "They're so detectable."

Jo winked at her other sisters. *"Delectable,* I think you mean."

"No need to act superior," Amy replied in a hurt voice. She took the newsprint from Meg and pointed to an article. "I noticed in the Pickwick Weekly Report that you aren't so very perfect. It says right here:

> 'Meg—good
> Jo—bad
> Beth—very good
> Amy—middling'

"Bethy's always very good. And everyone knows middling is better than bad," Amy added primly.

Jo jumped onto the couch, thrust her hands in

her pockets, and began to whistle as loudly as she could.

"Don't, Jo," Amy scolded, and covered her ears. "You sound so boyish."

"That's why I do it."

"I detest rude, unladylike girls!"

"I hate affected, niminy-piminy chits!"

"Don't peck at each other, children," said Beth. She made such a funny bird face that her sisters started laughing and for the moment forgot their quarrel.

Jo wandered to the window and rubbed away a small circle of frost with a corner of her sleeve. She peered through the falling snow down onto the street below. A fine carriage and a team of matching horses pulled into the drive of the house next door. A servant hurried from the house with an umbrella to shield an unsmiling, silver-haired gentleman and an awkward pale boy who stepped from the carriage. For an instant the boy gazed up toward the Marches' attic window and then disappeared inside the cheerless mansion.

"What do we think of the boy?" asked Jo over her shoulder to her sisters. "Is he a captive, like Smike in *Nicholas Nickleby?*"

Meg pushed Jo aside for a look out the window.

"He's had no upbringing at all, they say. He was reared in Italy among artists and vagrants."

"What's a vagrant?" Amy asked.

"Someone who is homeless, doesn't have a regular job or responsibilities, and roams where he pleases," Meg explained.

"Jehosephat!" Jo exclaimed. "Picture giving up freedom and excitement in Italy to come and live with that awful ancient grouch."

"Don't say *awful*. It's slang," Meg corrected her. She peered through the glass again. "Mr. Laurence intends to prepare the boy for business, and young Laurence stands to inherit his grandfather's entire firm."

Jo let out a great mouthful of air and sprawled face first on the couch. "Give me the artists and vagrants," she said dramatically.

Meg removed a ragged tea towel from a tray, revealing four unmatched cups, four chipped saucers, a sugar bowl, a steaming teapot, and a plate of toast cut in triangles and brushed with an ever-so-thin layer of what was left of last summer's raspberry preserves. "I shouldn't mind living in a fine house and having nice things," said Meg with a sigh. "Oh, it doesn't seem like Christmas this year, without presents."

"I'm desperate for drawing pencils," said Amy.

She pulled a chair close to the trunk and arranged a napkin in her lap. Always the domestic one, Beth carefully poured the tea into the cups.

"And you, Beth, what's your Christmas wish?" Meg asked.

Beth handed each sister a cup. "I'd like the war to end so Father can come home."

"Sweet Beth, we all want that," Jo replied. She nibbled each corner of her toast slowly to enjoy the raspberry taste—even the piece that fell on the floor and turned fuzzy with dust. "Say, do you hear the music coming from next door? It must be that Laurence boy playing again."

For a moment all four girls listened to the faint sound of a sad, faraway sonata. "Old Mr. Laurence does have a beautiful piano," Beth agreed.

"Wait till I'm a writer. I'll buy Beth the best piano in creation," Jo said.

Amy grabbed the biggest piece of remaining toast. "And if Jo doesn't become a writer, you can come over and play my piano, Beth. When I marry, I'm going to be disgustingly rich."

"And what if the one you love is a poor man, but good, like Father?" Meg asked.

Amy polished the back of a spoon against her knee and frowned at her reflection. "It isn't like being born with an ugly nose. You do have a choice about whom you love." She scraped barely half a teaspoonful of sugar from the cracked sugar bowl and dumped it all in her tea. "Belle Gardiner had four proposals. She'll never want for nice things."

Jo quickly gulped down the last of her tea. "I wouldn't marry for money. What if his business goes bust? Look what happened to Father. Besides, down at the *Eagle* they pay five dollars for every story they print. Why, I have ten stories in my head right now!"

Meg circled her empty teacup with one pale, elegant fingertip. "I dislike all this money talk. It isn't refined."

Amy popped the last bit of toast into her mouth and gave her oldest sister a wistful look. "We'll all grow up some day, Meg. We might as well know what we want."

Two

"Marmee! Marmee's home!" Beth shouted from the front entryway later that evening. The door flew open. In stepped the girls' mother, red faced, smiling, and covered with snow.

"You're frozen," Beth said after she gave Marmee a kiss on the cheek.

"Merry Christmas!" Marmee called, her bright blue eyes shining. Jo raced noisily down the steps ahead of Amy and Meg. She and her sisters gave their mother a hug. Meg took Marmee's ragtag woolen cloak and shook it. "Dear heart, thank you," Marmee said.

"We waited and waited!" wailed Amy. "We've been expectorating you for hours!"

"Expecting, featherhead," Jo said, and helped her mother take off her wet boots. Beth presented Marmee with her well-worn slippers, which had been warmed in front of the stove.

"Thank you, Cricket," Marmee said to Beth. "If you could see the people lined up outside Hope House in that bitter cold!"

"You finished the Christmas bundles?" Beth asked.

Marmee smoothed the front of her plain gray muslin dress and collapsed into a shabby, oversize chair in the parlor. Her daughters gathered around her. "There were so many this year. We were handing out food as quickly as we could make up the baskets."

Hannah, a stout, good-natured Irish woman, came from the kitchen with a cup of hot broth for Marmee. She had been the Marches' cook and housekeeper as long as any of the girls could remember. When Marmee was working long hours at Hope House, Hannah was often a great comfort to Jo and her sisters. "Thank you, Hannah," Marmee said. "You sent over a Mrs. Shaunnessy?"

"With the wee child?" Hannah asked. "Did you find something for the poor woman?"

"Triumph! Mrs. Chester on Church Street had need of a maid. A dollar a week and breakfast. And Mrs. Shaunnessy may bring her boy, if he's quiet and stays in the kitchen."

Jo sat cross-legged on the threadbare carpet at her mother's feet. "No doubt you had to be very clever to convince Mrs. Chester."

Marmee nodded mischievously. She patted her skirt pocket. "I've got a surprise for you, girls."

"A letter from Father!" Amy cried.

The girls made themselves comfortable. Meg perched on one chair arm, Amy on the other. Beth sat directly at Marmee's feet, while Jo leaned on the back of the chair in the shadow where no one could see her face in case Mr. March's precious letter was very sad.

"I think it was so splendid for Father to go as a chaplain to help with the religious services, especially when he's too old to be drafted and not strong enough for a soldier," said Meg.

"Don't I wish I could go as a drummer so I could be near him and help him," Jo replied.

"It must be very disagreeable to sleep in a tent and eat all sorts of bad-tasting things and drink out of a tin mug," Amy said.

"When will he come home, Marmee?" Beth asked quietly.

Marmee carefully unfolded the letter. "Not for many months, dear, unless he is sick. He will stay and do his work faithfully as he can, and we won't ask for him back a minute sooner than he can be spared. Now here's the letter.

" 'My Dearest Family, I am well and safe. Our battalion is encamped on the Potomac. December makes a hard cold season for all of us, so far from home. I pray that your own hardships will not be too great to bear. Give the girls all my dear love and a kiss. Tell them I think of them by day, pray for them by night, and find my best comfort in their affection. A year seems a very long time to wait before I see them. I know they will remember all I said to them, that they will be loving children to you, and that when I come back to them I may be fonder and prouder than ever of my little women.' "

Marmee took out a handkerchief, wiped her eyes, and blew her nose. The girls sniffed. Nobody spoke for a very long time. Jo brushed away a big tear before it dropped off the end of her nose. She missed her father and wondered how she would ever be able to do something that would make him proud.

"Shall we have a song before you go to bed?" Marmee asked, the way she did every night. The girls gathered around the old, out-of-tune piano, and Beth began to play. "'For the beauty of the earth, for the glory of the skies,'" they sang. "Lord of all, to thee we raise this, our hymn of grateful praise."

After they finished singing, the girls kissed Marmee good night and went to bed. But Jo couldn't sleep. She slipped upstairs to the attic with a candle. She opened the door to the attic closet, removed her special red velveteen writing cap and brown frock coat, and put them on. Then she took paper and pen from her special tin box. No bigger than a bread box, the tin container served as mouse-proof storage for Jo's manuscripts and supplies. She set to work, writing page after page. So busy was she creating fabulous, thrilling stories, she didn't see the family of mice scamper across the couch. She didn't even hear Marmee come up the steps and call, "Don't stay up too late, dear."

The next morning the yard was filled with marvelous white shapes. Jo woke up and peered out the window beside her bed. The hedgerow had become a parade of white elephants, and the bird bath was now a giant's wine goblet. How had such magic happened in one night? She rubbed her eyes and ran her hands through her tangled hair.

"Jo! Jo! Get out of bed!" Meg called from the stairs. "What miraculous food! You'll never believe what Hannah's made. It's just like the old days."

Jo jumped out of bed onto the cold floor and quickly dressed. When she came down the steps, she sniffed the air. "Do I smell sausages? Hannah, is this a Christmas miracle?" Jo waltzed the astonished Hannah around the dining room table. It was heaped with more good things to eat than any of the girls had seen in a very long time.

"Oh, butter!" Amy said, clasping her hands together as if in prayer. "God, thank you for this breakfast."

"And look here!" said Beth. She cupped an orange gently between her hands as if it were some precious gem. "We shouldn't eat it, we should just look at it."

"Jo, fetch your Marmee. She's down the alley behind Walden Street," Hannah said, handing Jo her cloak. "She went out early to see to some Germans named Hummel. They don't speak much English. Their da's gone and left six children with another one on the way." Hannah wiped her hands on her apron. Her expression softened. "Carry them a stick of firewood. Like as not, they ain't got any, nor breakfast neither."

Jo fastened her cloak and watched Hannah stomp back into the kitchen.

"Perhaps we could send the Hummels our bread," Beth said.

Her sisters looked startled when Jo picked up a loaf from the table. "Might as well take the butter. Butter's no good without bread to put it on."

To Jo's surprise, Amy offered the precious orange. Before long all four girls were packing up their Christmas breakfast to take to the Hummel family.

"What's going on here?" demanded Hannah as she carried a pot of porridge into the dining room. Jo winked and glided toward the door with the coffee pot. Behind her marched Meg with the plate of sausages and Amy and Beth with two armloads of firewood. Hannah slipped on her coat and followed with the steaming pot of porridge.

The sisters laughed and kicked up snow as they hurried along the street. "Wonderful snow!" Jo exclaimed. "Don't you wish we could roll around in it like dogs?"

On the Laurences' front porch stood old Mr. Laurence and the mysterious young man. Both were dressed for church and looked as if they were waiting for their carriage.

"Lovely weather for a picnic!" Jo shouted, and waved to their astonished-looking neighbors.

Beth giggled so hard she nearly dropped the kindling.

"Really, Jo!" whispered Meg. "You should let Mr. Laurence and his grandson speak first. What will they think of us? And whatever you do, don't look back."

The Laurence carriage clattered past the parade of March girls. The young man's curious face appeared in the rear window. It vanished when the carriage curtain was briskly shut.

"'. . . Love and joy come to you, and to you your wassail too!'" Jo and her sisters sang as loudly as they could on the quiet, snow-shrouded street. "'And God give you a happy new year!'"

After searching several alleys, the girls finally found the Hummels' small, ramshackle shed. It stood behind the dung heap of a neighboring stable. "Jehosephat!" Jo said softly.

"I've seen sheep living in a better place than this," Amy said.

Meg knocked. The door opened a crack, and a thin little girl's pale face poked through. Her hair was matted and filthy. Her lips were thin and bluish.

"Marmee? Are you in there? Are you all right?" Beth called anxiously.

The door swung wide, and Marmee beckoned the girls inside. "Look what you've brought!" she said, smiling. "Such Christmas cheer. Ah, my little women!"

Jo, her sisters, and Hannah stepped inside the smoky room that was so cramped and dark it took them a few minutes to become used to the lack of light. A woman with feverish-looking eyes lay on the only bed. Her face was streaked with sweat. Three small children huddled beside her under one miserable blanket.

"Shut the door and stoke up the fire, Beth," Marmee said.

"Ach, mein Gott! Good angels come to us!" The woman in the bed cried as Meg and Amy helped Hannah distribute the hot food.

"Funny angels in hoods and mittens," said Jo, and laughed. She had never been called an angel before and decided she liked the name. Marmee tipped a little lamp oil into one hand. She used the

19

tips of her fingers to expertly massage the tiny chest of a newborn wrapped in a bundle of rags on the table.

Jo had never seen such impossibly small fingers and toes before. "What will happen to this baby?" she whispered.

"God willing, he may live," Marmee replied quietly. She wrapped the child in her shawl and tucked him in bed beside his mother.

Jo leaned against a sooty wall and watched the Hummel children hop like hungry birds around her smiling sisters. The children devoured the bread and sausages and spoke rapidly in words Jo could not understand. It had been a Christmas of bewildering, disturbing contrasts, she thought. In one morning she had seen enchanting elephants made of snow and the haunting faces of starving children. What other surprises would the new year bring?

Three

*M*eg, what's the use of asking what we'll wear to Mrs. Gardiner's dance tonight?" Jo demanded. She took another big bite of apple and buried her head in her favorite book, *Pilgrim's Progress*. "You know we'll wear our poplin dresses because that's all we have."

Meg practiced a curtsy in front of the bedroom mirror. "There's nothing wrong in wishing we had real silk, is there?"

Jo shrugged and kept reading.

"You don't seem very excited about going to the New Year's Day party, Jo," complained Amy, who sat with Beth on the bed. "I'd give anything to see

Belle Gardiner and her engagement ring and what her nose looks like—"

"Her nose hasn't changed because she's getting married." Jo closed her book with a loud thump and stomped to the wardrobe.

"A nose can grow. Tremendously," Amy replied, touching her own nose with her fingers as if to check its size.

Jo held the maroon dress with the stiff white collar in front of herself. She scowled. "The front's all right, but I forgot about the burn and tear in the back."

"It's your own fault for always standing too close to the fire," Meg scolded. "Beth will patch the dress for you as best she can. When we get to the dance, you must sit still and keep your back out of sight." Meg pulled petticoats and stockings from the drawers. She found the little pearl pin Marmee had said she could borrow. "My gloves will do, though they're not as nice as I'd like. Stop making such a glum face, Jo. Where are your gloves?"

"Ruined," said Jo. She dangled the shriveled gloves in front of her sister's face. "I forgot about the time I spoilt them with lemonade."

"You are so careless!" Meg said with exasperation. "Gloves are more important than anything. A proper lady does not dance without gloves."

"I can crumple them up in my hand. Nobody will see the stains."

Meg shook her head and frowned.

"I know," Jo said brightly. "We'll each wear one good one and carry a bad one."

"Your hands are bigger than mine and you'll stretch my gloves," Meg said, and sighed. "Since there seems to be no other solution, I suppose I'll have to let you borrow them as long as you promise not to ruin them, too. And do behave nicely for once. Don't put your hands behind you, or stare, or say *Jehosephat*. It isn't ladylike."

"Don't worry about me," Jo said. "I'll be as civilized and proper as a stone statue in a cemetery."

Amy and Beth were quickly swept away by the excitement of helping their older sisters get ready for the dance. They scurried up and down the stairs to fetch this and that.

"What cunning little heels, Meg!" exclaimed Amy when she found some hand-me-down green satin slippers. "They're from one of the Emerson girls. I hope they won't be at the party, will they?"

Meg struggled to squeeze her feet into the

embroidered shoes. "They're drastically small, but rather smart. It's only for one night. I don't think anyone will remember that Louise Emerson wore them last year."

Amy handed Meg a hand mirror. "Curls around your face would be very flattering," Amy suggested.

"Do you think so?" Meg asked.

"I'll fix your hair for you," Jo volunteered. She hurried downstairs to the kitchen to heat metal tongs on the stove. When the tongs were red hot, she brought them back upstairs. Then she wound paper around strands of Meg's hair and clamped the tongs tight.

"Are the curls supposed to smoke like that?" Beth asked.

"Whew!" said Amy, holding her nose. "What a smell!"

"It's just the dampness drying," Jo said with authority.

"Reminds me of burnt feathers," Amy said, and flounced her own natural curls.

"Just as soon as I take off these papers you'll see a cloud of lovely little ringlets," Jo promised. But when she unclamped the tongs, out came almost all of Meg's lovely bangs.

"Oh, what have you done? I'm bald!" Meg wailed when she poked her hand through the remaining ragged frizzle standing straight up on her head. "I can't go out like this!"

"Good," Jo said, biting her lip. "I'm not going, either."

Meg buried her face in her arm and sobbed. "I'll never have any suitors. I'll just die an old maid."

"There, there, Meg. We'll tie a bow in front so it will look very becoming," said Amy, coming to the rescue with her own green hair ribbon. "You don't need lots of suitors. You only need one if he's the right one."

"Meg isn't going to be married right away, is she?" Beth asked in alarm.

"She's never getting married," Jo replied.

"With your help, I never will," Meg said angrily.

"I *am* sorry about your hair," Jo said in a low voice. "I always spoil everything."

"Well, it can't be helped now," Beth said. "Come on, Jo and Meg, it's nearly time to go."

When the girls were finally dressed and ready, they made their way down the front steps carrying one good glove and one bad while Marmee, Amy, and Beth watched from the hall below. Meg looked very pretty in the green dress with Amy's matching ribbon. For once, Jo did not clunk loudly down the stairs. She walked slowly and kept her head perfectly still so that her long hair, twisted in a corkscrew on the back of her head, would not come undone.

"Bravo!" exclaimed Beth and Amy.

"You both look lovely," Marmee said.

"Well, I don't feel lovely. My head aches," Jo complained. "All nineteen hair pins are sticking straight into my brain. My feet are so tangled in this long skirt, I'll never be able to jump a fence."

"Have you a nice handkerchief?" Marmee called as the girls bundled up in woolen cloaks and scarves.

"Yes, Marmee!" Meg replied.

Jo giggled when she shut the door behind them. "She'd ask us that even if we were running away from an earthquake."

Laughter and the gay music of a string quartet floated across the lawn from the Gardiners' house as Jo and Meg walked closer. "Now, mind you don't eat much supper. And *don't* shake hands with people, it isn't the thing anymore," Meg said in a low voice. "And most of all, don't forget about your dress."

Jo gulped. Her hands began to sweat. How could

she remember so many rules? And what if she made a terrible mistake?

"Come on, Jo," Meg said. "I have a wonderful feeling about tonight."

"I don't," Jo mumbled. She did not say anything when a servant took her cloak and handed her and Meg dance programs. Inside the small white paper booklets were spaces for each dance to be penciled in with the names of partners. While a group of eager boys quickly filled in Meg's program, Jo slunk away with her back carefully hidden. She wadded up her empty program and stuck it in a potted palm.

The music played and everyone seemed to be having a lovely time. Everyone except Jo. She peeked into the parlor, where the elegant mahogany chairs had been pushed against the wall to make room for dancing. A group of girls her age gathered around Belle Gardiner. They clustered in a cloud of yellow silk and blue-and-white crinoline.

"Diamonds, rubies, and sapphires!" one girl shrieked.

"It's the most magnificent thing I've ever seen," another said.

Jo left the parlor in disgust. She leaned against the hallway wall, bored and lonely. A polka played.

Jo couldn't help herself. She tapped her foot and hummed. Out of the corner of her eye, she noticed Mrs. Gardiner standing beside a gawky boy with red hair. Mrs. Gardiner gestured with her fan in Jo's direction.

Panic-stricken, Jo scooted sideways along the wall in search of a place to hide. There! She dove into a doorway hung with red velvet drapery. On the other side she crashed into something solid.

The Laurence boy.

Jo staggered backward in embarrassment.

"Hello!" he said, grinning sheepishly. He held a dish of French ice that looked as if it might escape onto the carpeting any minute. "You're welcome to hide here, too."

"Jehosephat! I'm sorry!" Jo exclaimed, and tried to scramble out from behind the curtain.

"No, please stay! I just came here so I could stare at people."

Jo glanced curiously at the smiling boy with the smear of French ice on his cheek. He had straight brown hair, large hazel eyes, and a handsome nose. Jo noted that he was taller than she was. He seemed very polite and friendly for a boy and altogether jolly compared to everyone else at the party. She wondered how old he was.

"Should I put on my jacket?" he whispered. His tie was loose, and his jacket lay rolled in a heap on the floor. "I never know the rules here. I'm Laurie—Theodore Laurence, but I'm called Laurie."

"Jo March," Jo said, and put out her hand as if to shake his hand. At the last minute she remembered Meg's advice and withdrew it. "Who were you staring at?"

"You, actually. What game were you playing?"

"I don't know, but I think I won." Jo laughed, pleased. "Who else were you watching?"

"I'm quite taken with that one," he said. They both peeked out through the drapery.

"Belle Gardiner? She's engaged."

"Not Miss Gardiner. The very beautiful one with the lovely eyes."

"That's Meg. My sister," Jo said, then added slyly, "She's completely bald in front."

Laurie looked at Jo in surprise. Now that she had his complete attention, she asked, "Did you really live in Italy among artists and vagrants?"

"My mother was Italian. A pianist. Grandfather disapproved of her."

"Truly? I saw a play like that. Do you like the theater?"

"Well, yes—"

"Were you born there?"

"Where? Oh, Italy—"

"Do you speak French or Italian?" Jo asked in the rapid-fire manner she used when she wanted to find out everything she could about someone.

"I speak English at home and French at school. *Parlez-vous français?"* he asked with a grin.

Jo shook her head, picked up his spoon, and took a bite of his ice. He did not seem to mind. "What school?"

"The Conservatory of Music in Vevey. Grandfather's having me tutored now. He insists I go to college." Laurie frowned.

"I'd commit murder to go to college," Jo said. A spoonful of ice slipped and fell on her sleeve. She wiped it with her sister's glove. "Actually I'm going to Europe."

"Really?"

"Well, I mean I *hope* I'm going to Europe," Jo said, embarrassed to be caught by her own lie. "My great-aunt March says she'll go one day, and she has to take me. I work as her companion."

"You're not in school?"

"No, I'm a businessman—girl, I should say. Meg is, too." Jo finished off the ice and licked the spoon. "You must have heaps of books. Do you read a lot? I have to read to Aunt March, hours and hours. I do all the voices for all the characters in the stories."

Laurie grinned. "I'll bet you do."

"If I weren't going to be a famous writer, I'd go to New York and become an actress. Are you shocked?"

"Very," Laurie replied, still smiling. He put out his elbow and motioned for Jo to take his arm. "Would you like to dance?"

"I can't," Jo said, shaking her head. "I told Meg I wouldn't because—"

"Because what?" Laurie asked curiously.

"You won't tell?"

"Never!"

"Well, I have a bad trick of standing before the fire and so I burn my frocks, and I scorched this one. Meg ordered me to keep still so no one would see it. You may laugh if you want. It is funny, I know."

Laurie didn't laugh. He made a gallant bow and said gently, "Never mind. We'll dance in the long hall where no one can see us."

Overjoyed, Jo took Laurie's arm. Together they danced a spirited, clumsy polka up and down the hallway. Jo hooted with laughter. "Sorry! At home, Meg makes me take the gentleman's part," Jo apologized as she crashed into him again. "It's a shame you don't know the lady's part. Are you looking at the back of my skirt? You cheat!"

"It doesn't look so bad, honestly."

"You promised you wouldn't look." She and Laurie stumbled, hobbled, and crashed to the end of the hallway. They stopped abruptly. Huddled on the steps was Meg, holding her ankle and making a miserable face. "What's the matter?" Jo asked.

"I think I've sprained my ankle," Meg said pitifully.

"I shouldn't wonder," Laurie replied, "in those slippers."

Meg jutted out her bottom lip, clearly angered by his criticism of her shoes.

"Does it hurt?" Laurie asked. He knelt for a better look.

Meg primly pulled her foot out of sight beneath her long skirt. "Gentlemen aren't supposed to look at a lady's limbs."

Jo guffawed. "This isn't a gentleman. This is our neighbor, Laurie, the captive. Now be honest, tell us how you feel."

"Horrible," Meg said. Her eyes filled with tears. "A perfectly good party, ruined."

"I'll go tell Mrs. Gardiner," Jo suggested.

"No!" Meg exclaimed. "She'll think I've been sampling the wine punch."

"But how will we get home?" Jo asked.

"I'll give you both a ride in my carriage. It's no problem at all," Laurie said politely.

When the girls arrived at home, they were greeted by Marmee and their sisters. Marmee immediately went to work on Meg's swollen ankle with her kit of medical supplies.

"You two have all the luck riding home in the Laurence boy's carriage," Amy announced in a nasal twang. Her voice sounded strange because of the clothespin she had clipped to her nose to improve its shape. "Is he very romantic?"

"Not in the slightest," Jo said, helping Meg to a chair in the kitchen.

"He's a dreadful boy." Meg winced as her mother touched her ankle.

"Well, he did a good deed, putting ice on this," Marmee said. "Now go to bed, Amy."

"He put ice on your ankle? With his own hands?" Amy asked.

"Oh, stop being so swoony," Jo replied. She

couldn't understand why her sister acted so silly. "You mustn't be soppy about Laurie, any more than you'd be soppy about a dog or a chair. I hope we shall be friends with him."

"With a boy?" Amy said in horror.

"He isn't a boy," Jo insisted. "He's Laurie."

Four

~⌒~

On the first day of February, Jo, Meg, and Amy hurried out of the house into the cold, overcast morning. "Blast these wretched long skirts!" Jo said, struggling through a drift of snow.

"Don't say *blast* and *wretched*," Amy scolded. She stamped her feet and clutched her school slate.

"I like good strong words," said Jo. She gathered up a handful of snow with her mittens. "It's perfect for packing. Look at this snowball."

"Don't make us late again, Jo," Amy said. "Aunt March will be vexed, and I'll be in terrible trouble with Mr. Davis."

"Don't forget about me. I'll get a scolding, and I

might lose my job taking care of those four horrid King brats," said Meg. "Jo, where do you think you're going? Come back here."

Jo paid no attention to her sister and leapt across the untrampled snow in Mr. Laurence's yard. She took careful aim and threw the snowball directly at the second-floor window she hoped was Laurie's. For a moment she held her breath. What if she broke the glass? Old Mr. Laurence would never forgive her.

Splat! The snowball hit the sill.

The window opened. "Hello!" cried Laurie. He leaned out and waved. "Come and visit. It's dull as tombs up here."

"Can't," Jo bellowed.

"Come away this instant," Meg hissed at her sister. "Stop shouting. You sound like you're calling a cow."

Jo ignored her sister and made a mock curtsey in Laurie's direction. "We're on our way to employment and Mr. Davis's School for Young Ladies."

"I'd come down and have another snowball fight but my tutor won't let me," Laurie said with a grin. "I beat you square and fair last time."

"Did not," Jo replied.

"Did, too," Laurie said, and laughed loudly.

"But I know there's no arguing with you, Miss March."

"The whole neighborhood can hear you," Amy said.

"I'll visit later, if you'd like," Jo boomed. "How about ice skating again?"

"Terrific!" Laurie shouted, and waved. "Meet you at the river at five o'clock. And tell Meg that my tutor, Mr. John Brooke, sends his greetings."

Meg blushed and began walking angrily up the elm-lined sidewalk with Amy. Jo lifted her skirt in a most unladylike fashion and loped over the drifts to catch up with them.

"Well, I've never!" Meg sputtered. "Of all the rude displays."

"I had to shout," Jo said, trying to make peace. "How else could Laurie have heard me up on the second floor?"

"I'm not talking about *that,* although your behavior was abominable. Imagine telling someone to shout down good day. Such manners!" Meg exclaimed as they stopped in front of the Kings' fine brick Georgian house.

Jo shrugged. Laurie's tutor always seemed perfectly agreeable, if a bit stiff and formal to her. She didn't like the way he stopped to talk to Meg in his moony, serious kind of manner. He was always leaving his calling card on the front plate in the hall and lingering to tip his hat whenever they passed on the boardwalk in town. There was no reason for him to go through all that trouble. Perhaps he was lonely, although Jo couldn't think why. Laurie was quite an amusing fellow, once a person got to know him.

"You are impossible, Jo," Meg said, and sighed. "Perhaps if I'm lucky this morning Mrs. King will have already left to make social calls and I won't have to listen to her lecture about tardiness."

"Well, I'd certainly trade places with you, Meg," Amy said. "Why do I have to go to school anyhow? I'm so daguerrogated I can hardly hold my head up. I owe at least a dozen limes."

"Limes?" Jo said, and rolled her eyes.

"Are limes the fashion now?" Meg asked.

"Of course," Amy replied. "It's nothing but limes. Everyone keeps them in their desks and trades them for beads and things. All the girls treat one another at recess. If you don't bring limes to school, you're nothing. You might as well be dead. I've had ever so many, and I can't pay anyone back."

Jo wrapped her cloak tightly about herself. "No wonder you never learn anything at that school."

Meg glanced once more at the King house and

untied a corner of her handkerchief. "Here, Amy. Take this quarter. Marmee gave me the rag money this month. I know what it feels like to do without any little luxuries, but we are not destitute." Joyously, Amy threw her arms around her sister.

Jo would have none of it. The fad seemed a perfect waste of money. She could think of a hundred books she'd rather buy than spend money on limes. In disgust she left her sisters and strode off to Aunt March's house.

The gleaming mahogany grandfather clock in the hall at Plumfield Estate struck one o'clock. Jo yawned. For the past two hours she had been trapped in Aunt March's fussy, airless parlor with the fans and feathers on the walls, the china gimcracks and bric-a-brac statues filling the shelves. Every space, from the mantel to the top of the piano, was crammed with sea shells and vases and candlesticks. Crocheted tidies and doilies decorated the backs and arms of the overstuffed armchairs and matching settee. On the walls were sad-eyed pictures called *Trout* and *Mother and Child.*

"Go on! Keep reading!" Aunt March yelped. "I'm not paying you to stare into space."

Jo cleared her throat and picked up the book

again. " 'Secondly, the immortality of the soul is asserted to be in consequence of its immateriality as in all leipothymic cases,' " she droned on and on. After a while her aunt stopped petting the small white poodle in her lap. The dog had fallen asleep. Her aunt's wide, fleshy chin sank low on her lace-covered chest, and she began to snore, too. Jo had never noticed before how much Aunt March reminded her of the scowling painted china pug dog that guarded the parlor fireplace.

Quietly Jo tiptoed across the thick carpet. She slipped *David Copperfield* from the crowded bookshelf. Before she could take a more comfortable seat on the window-seat cushion and begin reading, she glanced out the window. She noticed someone standing by the tall, wrought-iron gate. Amy! What was she doing out of school so soon? And why was she crying?

Jo flew out of the parlor. The poodle and Aunt March startled awake. The little dog skittered after Jo and yapped and jumped in the hallway. "Josephine, there's a draft," Aunt March called.

But Jo was all the way down the sidewalk. "What's wrong?" Jo asked breathlessly. "Is it Father?"

Amy shook her head and wept.

Jo breathed a great sigh of relief. "Something at school?"

Amy nodded. Miserably, she held up her lovely hand to show a red welt across the back of it.

"That teacher ought to be arrested at once!" Jo said angrily. "And if not arrested, then strangled."

"It was about the limes," Amy blubbered. "May Chester told him I had a whole packet of them in my desk. They're not allowed, you know, but everyone brings them. Mr. Davis decided to make me the example. He hit me with his pointer in front of everyone. I've never been so embarrassed in my life."

"There, there," Jo said, stroking the top of her sister's head. "Marmee will know what to do. We'll go home and tell her right now."

Jo made her excuses to Aunt March, who was none too pleased to have Jo's day cut short. "There's always some catastrophe in your family," she grumbled. "You may go, but mind you come early tomorrow to make up for the time. I am not running a charity here, you know."

When the girls arrived home, Marmee paced furiously across the kitchen floor. "By law Mr. Davis may beat his pupils freely—as well as his children and his wife and his horse, for that matter."

"There must be something we can do," Jo insisted. "It's an appalling school. Amy knew more going in than she knows now."

Amy looked up from the basin of rose glycerin in which she was soaking her hand. "That's not true!"

"Yes it is," Jo insisted. "You begged to go there with those silly girls, and now you've forgotten everything Father taught you. Your spelling's atrocious, your Latin's absurd."

Amy sighed and said in a small voice, "Mr. Davis told us it's as useful to educate a woman as it is to educate a female cat."

"He did, did he?" Marmee said with new fury. She took out a sheet of paper and a pen. "I'm writing that man a letter of complaint about his brutal use of punishment. That's the last time he'll use one of the March girls to set an example. Anyone who hits and humiliates a child is only teaching that child to hit and humiliate in turn."

Amy's face filled with hope. "You mean I don't have to go back?"

"That's right. I'm withdrawing you from that school at once."

Amy cried for joy. "No more lessons! Thank you, thank you, Marmee—"

"Not so fast, young lady," Marmee continued. "Your education is not over."

Amy looked disappointed.

"If you can promise to discipline yourself and govern your vanities, I will ask Jo if she will help you with your lessons here at home. Do you agree, Jo?"

Jo nodded. She was pleased Marmee thought her responsible enough to teach her youngest sister, especially when she knew that Amy loved gossip more than grammar.

"Do you agree, Amy?"

Amy nodded halfheartedly.

"You have a good many little gifts and virtues, Amy," Marmee continued. "But there is no need parading them, any more than you would dress up in all your gowns, bonnets, and ribbons all at once just to show folks you have them." Marmee gently patted Amy's hand dry with a towel, then kissed her forehead.

After supper that night, Jo put on her red velvet writing cap and climbed the stairs to the attic with a candle. While she scratched away in her copybook, Beth tiptoed into the room and looked over Jo's shoulder.

"I know you're here, Bethy. You're no good at sneaking about like the mice," Jo said with a laugh.

"Is the story good?" Beth asked good-naturedly.

Jo scratched her cheek and left behind an ink smudge. "Don't know. It's all murder and gore." She handed the copybook to Beth, stood up, and restlessly shuffled toward the frost-covered window. "You're the only one I can tell this to because you're the only one who understands."

"What?"

"I don't think I'll ever be like Marmee," Jo confided, turning toward her sister. "The fact is that I rather crave violence. If only I could go to war like Father and right wrongs and stand up to the lions of injustice."

"And so Marmee does, in her own way."

"But I want to do something splendid. Something that turns the world upside down."

"Perhaps you will," Beth said, smiling at her sister.

Five

~~~

One evening a few days later, a bell sounded in the attic. *Dong!* Two old sheets pinned to a clothesline flew apart, revealing a castle tower in a gloomy wood made from old furniture and boxes stacked and covered with a quilt. At the top of the tower stood a flag made of a stick and a handkerchief. The only light came from smoky candles arranged in tin cans on the floor.

Onstage knelt Lady Violet, played by Meg in Marmee's old lavender shawl. Countess de Montanescu, performed by Beth in an old black, hooded cloak, stood before her with a curiously furry baby in her arms.

"Meeooooow!" cried Mrs. Pat-Paw, an unwilling actress in a doll's bonnet and dress.

"Go on! Say your lines, Lady Violet, before the baby leaps out the window and down a tree," prompted Jo, who was stage manager, playwright, and Duke of Gloucester in a horsehair beard.

"Oh, dear Countess, pray for me!" said Lady Violet. "I have sinned against myself and my brother Roderigo!"

Jo smacked her forehead with the heel of her hand. She sat down on a crate in the audience and waved the script in exasperation. "Say 'sinned' as if you mean it!"

Meg tried again, this time with more wicked pleasure.

"Roderigo!" Jo bellowed. "Where are you? You're supposed to be onstage seeking the Duke of Gloucester."

"You don't have to yell," complained Amy as Roderigo. She stomped onstage in a boy's pants and vest, a dented tin pot on her head.

"Hark ye," Jo announced, jumping to her feet as the duke. She flourished her favorite pasteboard sword in the air, "Who goes there?"

Meg banged a pot lid on cue. No one answered.

"Hark ye! Who goes there?" Jo repeated. "Roderigo!"

Roderigo clutched the tilting tin pot hat. "I am thirsty. Give me something to drink, Duke!"

The duke smiled an evil sneer and poured something into a cracked cup. "Here, Roderigo."

Roderigo took a pretend sip, staggered a few steps, and lowered himself carefully to the ground without spilling a drop.

Jo rolled her eyes. "You've just been poisoned, Amy! Can't you act like it?"

"I don't want to fall down and get all black and blue with bruises," Amy complained.

"Watch me. This is how it should be done," Jo said. She swept the cup to her lips, took a sip, threw the remaining liquid over her shoulder, and let out an ear-piercing scream. She tore her hair, clutched her throat, staggered across stage, knocked down part of the castle tower, and plunged to the floor with a thud, stone-cold dead.

Meg and Beth cheered.

"See?" Jo said, revived by the applause. "You try it."

"Oh, all right," said Amy. She picked up the poison, took a ladylike sip, stepped to the left, stepped to the right, then wavered and lowered herself onto a couch cushion on the floor.

Jo howled with impatience. She pulled on her beard and paced back and forth before the stage.

"I want to be Lady Violet," Amy said. "I'm exhaustified of being the boy."

Meg and Beth groaned. "We've already had this argument a hundred times," Meg complained. "You're too little to be Lady Violet."

Beth handed Mrs. Pat-Paw to Amy. By now the cat had clawed off her bonnet. "Here. You can be the Countess de Montanescu."

"You don't have any lines," Amy said in an ungrateful voice. "And then who will play Roderigo?"

Jo rapped the floor with her pasteboard sword. "Gentlemen, I propose the admission of a new member to our theatrical society. Just the person we need for our operatic tragedy—Theodore Laurence."

"What?" Meg said in shock. "That boy?"

"He'll laugh at our acting and make fun of us later," Amy said. "We've never allowed boys here before. Ever."

"He'll think we're silly," Beth whispered.

"No, he won't, upon my word as a gentleman," Jo protested.

Meg removed her lavender shawl. "Jo, when it's only ladies, we don't guard our conduct in the same way."

Amy nodded. "We bare our souls and tell our most appalling secrets. He'll find us improper."

"Oh, please. Let's try him. He's wanted to join us for ever so long," Jo pleaded.

The attic closet door flew open. Jo's sisters screamed. Out jumped Laurie, red faced and laughing. Amy, Beth, and Meg ran for cover behind the scenery.

"Jo, you traitor!" Meg cried from under the castle. "How could you? He heard everything."

Mrs. Pat-Paw yowled and fled down the stairs. Laurie made a low bow. "Fellow artists, may I present myself as an actor, musician, and loyal and *very* humble servant of the Pickwick Society."

"We'll be the judge of that," Jo said with mock gruffness. Beth, Amy, and Meg poked their heads out from behind the quilt and giggled.

"In token of my gratitude and as a means of promoting communication between adjoining nations—shouting from windows being forbidden—I shall provide a post office in our hedge." Laurie grandly displayed the "post office" from the closet where he had been hiding. It was an old, white birdhouse with a red roof that lifted on hinges. "I promise never to reveal what I receive in confidence inside this post office." He put his hand to his heart to show he meant every word.

Jo's sisters seemed so impressed by his earnestness, they clapped their hands and cheered. Meg handed Laurie a copy of the script. Amy gave him the dented tin pot hat.

"Take your place, Roderigo," Jo said with delight. And the operatic tragedy rehearsal began once more.

The next morning Jo felt very strange. She got up early, before anyone else in the house was awake, tiptoed outside, and scanned the early dawn sky. The snow had not melted, and the robins had not returned. Yet she had a restless, hungry feeling that spring was coming. She sniffed the cold air as she walked along a path in the woods not far from her house. It smelled of pine trees and mystery.

She loosened her boot laces, shook down her hair so that it fell free about her shoulders, and tied her coat about her waist. Then she set off as fast as she could down the path. Her hair streaming, the wind in her face, she lifted her skirt and hurdled a narrow frozen stream. On and on she ran until she found herself back at the hedge between her house and the Laurence place. What was that? Something was sticking out of the roof of the birdhouse! She opened the roof and gave a cry of joy.

"Four tickets to the theater," she whispered to herself. *"The Seven Castles of Diamond Lake.* A real show! Ah, thank you, Laurie. Thank you!"

She hurried into the house and found her sisters eating breakfast. "Where have you been? Your hair's a mess," Meg said, handing Jo a bowl of porridge.

"Look what was inside the post office in the hedge," Jo said, waving the tickets and a yellow note in the air. "Four tickets to the theater tonight. There's a note that says the tickets are for me, Laurie, Mr. Brooke, and Meg. How do you like that? Isn't that grand?"

"Wonderful!" Beth said with real enthusiasm.

Jo suddenly felt guilty. "I'm sorry you weren't invited, Beth."

"Not at all," Beth replied. "The two eldest should go. That's you and Meg. I know you'll have a wonderful time."

"What about me?" Amy said, and pouted. "I want to go to the theater, too. I never get to go anywhere."

"You're too little," Jo said. She ate her porridge so fast she burned her mouth.

"I'm not little. You're just hogging Laurie," Amy insisted.

Jo ignored her youngest sister. "What do you think, Meg? Aren't you excited?"

Meg seemed distracted. She gazed into space with a strange dreamy expression on her face. "I hope my dress won't look too shabby."

"Jehosephat, Meg, it isn't a coronation!" Jo exclaimed. "It's just Laurie and awful Mr. Brooke."

Meg gave Jo a hurt look. She rose from the table and quickly cleared the bowls. "Come on, now, we're going to be late for work, Jo."

"Can't you ask Laurie for another ticket?" Amy pleaded.

"No," Jo said firmly, and buttoned her cloak around her neck. "You're weeks behind in algebra, Amy. Today while I'm gone at Aunt March's, I want you to finish the pages I've marked. I won't have a sister who's a lazy ignoramus. And don't sulk. You look like a pigeon."

Beth filled the basin with steaming water from the kettle and began washing the breakfast dishes. "I promise to keep my eye on your pupil, Jo."

"You'll be sorry for this, Jo March!" Amy said between clenched teeth.

After the play that night, Meg and Jo returned to the house full of high spirits. "Didn't Mrs. Nell Watson swoon wonderfully?" Jo said. "What a spectacular performance! I wish we had half the costumes and scenery in our theater upstairs."

Meg leaned dreamily against the wall, still in her cloak.

"What's wrong with you?" Jo said, alarmed by her sister's strange expression. Jo's eyes narrowed. "I hope you haven't caught anything from Mr. Brooke. You certainly plastered yourself against him enough this evening."

Meg glared at Jo. "It's proper to take a gentleman's arm if it's offered."

" 'I confess I'm distracted at the theater,' " Jo lisped, imitating John Brooke's voice. " 'What peculiar lives actresses must lead.' Jehosephat!"

"Be quiet!" Meg said, her face bright red. "Thanks to you, I thought I'd die when Laurie announced to Mr. Brooke that I adored the theater. What if Laurie tells Mr. Brooke about our wild theatricals in the attic? I'll never be able to show my face in front of him again."

"Laurie won't tell. He's bound to secrecy," Jo replied hotly. "And since when do you care so much about what dull Mr. Brooke thinks?"

Meg refused to answer. She pitched her cloak on the hall-stand hook, stomped upstairs, and slammed the bedroom door.

"Jo?" Marmee called from the parlor. "What's all the fuss about?"

Jo trudged into the room and gave her mother a kiss on the cheek. "Just a difference of opinion, that's all," Jo said sullenly. She collapsed onto the sagging horsehair sofa. "The play was wonderful. Meg wasn't."

Marmee looked up from the desk where she was writing. "What's wrong?"

"She doesn't share secrets anymore. She doesn't laugh at my jokes," Jo complained. "One minute she's weeping, the next she's giggling. I want things to be the way they were. I want the old Meg back."

Marmee stood up and came to the sofa to sit beside Jo.

"The other day," Jo whispered, "I caught her singing and waltzing around the kitchen with a broom. Last night I caught her talking to herself in front of the mirror. Before we left for the play, she moped in the corner. She's twittery and cross. She doesn't eat. What's the matter with her? Is she ill?"

"She's perfectly fine," Marmee said gently. "She's just in love."

"In love?" Jo exploded. "What's perfectly fine about that? How could she do this to us? I can't believe it—" She stopped and sniffed the air. "Marmee, do you smell something burning? Jehosephat! It's coming from upstairs. The candles!"

Marmee leapt to her feet. Jo sprinted ahead up the steps. When she arrived in the attic she saw a small fire smoldering inside the tin box. "My manuscript!" Jo said in anger and disbelief as she watched *The Lost Duke of Gloucester* smolder. "Who would have done such a thing?"

Marmee poured water from a pitcher into the box. Bitter smoke rose in the air. All that remained of Jo's work was soggy, blackened shreds.

"What's going on?" Amy asked, coughing innocently. She climbed out from behind the couch.

"You did this!" Jo shouted angrily.

Amy nimbly ran down the steps, dove into her bedroom, and locked the door. Jo pounded on the door. "I'll hate you as long as I live!" Jo shouted, tears streaming down her face.

"Amy!" Marmee called. "Open that door at once."

As soon as the door opened, Jo jumped on her

younger sister and began slapping and shaking her in a wild rage. Marmee managed to wrench the girls apart. "Girls, stop!"

"You're not my sister," Jo screamed. "You're nothing, you're dead!"

Amy was scolded severely by her mother. But it took nearly an hour for Marmee and Beth to calm Jo. "It was a great loss," Marmee said as Jo lay sobbing in her bed, "and you've every right to be put out. But don't let the sun go down on your anger. Forgive each other, and begin again tomorrow."

Jo shook her head. "I'll never forgive her. Never."

Six

〜

*T*he next day Jo still felt angry and unforgiving. She decided to go ice skating with Laurie. Everybody's so hateful at home, Jo thought. Laurie's the only one who knows how to cheer me up.

The early evening sky was dull gray when they set off for the frozen Concord River. Jo sat on a rail fence along the riverbank to strap her skates onto the bottom of her boots. "Race you to the red scarf that's tied to that tree! See it?" Jo said. She stood on the ice and twirled in little circles while Laurie finished putting on his skates.

"Be careful, Jo. See all that weak ice? This is our

last chance to skate before the thaw." Laurie threw a fallen limb to mark a black, dangerous section where the river had bubbled through. He and Jo toed up, shoulder to shoulder. "Ready, get set— *go!"* he cried, and sped around the bend.

Jo hesitated, lost her balance, and glanced over her shoulder in time to see a striped red-and-white wool hat bobbing along the riverbank. "Wait for me!" Amy cried as she struggled to catch up.

She'll ruin everything, Jo thought. I'll pretend I don't see her. She dashed off toward Laurie in long, confident strides and grabbed his coattail to slow him down.

"No fair!" Laurie called over his shoulder.

"Race you to the trees!" Jo said, laughing.

"Keep near the shore. Stay away from the middle," Laurie called over his shoulder.

The ice made a wonderful *tock-tock-tock* noise as Jo's gleaming skates bit the surface. She felt strangely satisfied abandoning her sister. I hope she's miserable, Jo thought. Serves her right.

As Jo reached the bend, she slowed and looked back again. Suddenly an ear-splitting crack filled the air. Splash! The red-and-white cap vanished.

"Amy!" Jo tried to scream. Nothing but a whisper came from her lips. She tried to move her legs. Nothing happened. There wasn't a moment to lose. How would she save her sister?

Someone whizzed past, jolting her back into action. "Get a fence rail and throw it to me!" Laurie shouted.

Jo sped to shore and grabbed a fence rail. "Catch!" She pitched the rail toward Laurie, who had already grabbed a branch and was skating swiftly toward the hole in the ice.

The ice groaned beneath Jo's feet. She skidded to a stop, her heart beating wildly. Carefully, she lowered herself to her knees and stretched out flat on her stomach. She snaked a few feet. The ice cracked. Would it hold? She held her breath and kept moving toward the place where Laurie was kneeling.

When she finally made it to the break in the ice, she could see Amy's small, bare hand splash above the water's surface. Laurie held out the branch. "Grab hold!" he called.

"Can't!" Amy cried. She thrashed in the water and disappeared. When she reemerged, he held out the rail. She lunged for it but missed again.

"Do something!" Jo screamed. She knelt over the hole with Laurie. Together they managed to grab Amy's arm, snag her coat, and pull her out of the water. Amy flopped, gasping and soaking, on to solid ice.

"Wrap her in this," Laurie said, and struggled to remove his coat.

Amy's blue lips shivered. Her teeth chattered. "I can't feel my legs."

Jo stripped off her own woolen skirt, leaving on only her bloomers. She bundled her skirt around Amy's wet legs. Carefully, Laurie and Jo slid Amy back across the safe sections of ice. As soon as they reached the shore, they tugged away the straps of their skates. Laurie picked up Amy and raced through the woods toward home. Jo followed close behind.

Somehow they managed to carry Amy home, shivering, dripping, and crying. Marmee met them at the door and wrapped the little girl in blankets before the fire. Jo was too frightened to speak, too frightened to think. She darted here and there, warming tea, finding a hot-water bottle, heaping her sister with one blanket after another.

Jo's hands were cut and bruised by the splintery rail and stubborn skate straps. Her hair was wild, her face pale. Only when Amy dozed off did she dare ask her mother, "Is she going to die?"

Marmee shook her head. She smiled gently and hung Jo's skirt and coat up before the fire. "I think she'll be all right. You were wise to cover her and get her home quickly."

"Laurie was the one who rescued her," Jo said, full of sorrow as she looked at her sister's sleeping face. "If she dies, it will be all my fault."

Meg tiptoed into the room and handed Jo a blanket. In a mock scolding voice she said, "Josephine March, I can't believe you walked all the way home in your bloomers."

Jo smiled weakly and wrapped the blanket around herself. She moved closer to the fire. One of Mrs. Pat-Paw's kittens jumped into Amy's lap, circled once, and began to purr. Amy opened her eyes.

"I'm so sorry," Jo said in a low voice, leaning close to her sister. "I'm so horrible."

"No," said Amy, "I'm sorry. I'm much more horribler than you."

Jo stroked her sister's hair. "What if you'd drowned? What if Laurie hadn't been there?"

Amy's face grew suddenly sad. "Jo, do you love Laurie more than you love me?"

"Don't be such a beetle," Jo said with a gentle laugh. "I'll never love anyone as I love my sisters." She squeezed Amy's hand, glad to feel the warm, familiar softness again.

Later that evening Jo put on her red velveteen

writing cap. But instead of climbing up into the attic, she perched on Amy's bed. There, surrounded by comforters and kittens and all of Beth's favorite armless and legless dolls, Jo read to her sister from her copybook. "How did that scene sound?"

"Very good except we've left out the best part. Remember what happened before that?" Amy said. "Lady Ann falls in love with the duke's rival."

"That's right. Yes, the grotto scene," Jo said and began scribbling away furiously. With Amy's help, she was determined to reconstruct the story that had been destroyed in the fire.

"I adore the grotto scene," Amy said.

"I do, too," Jo replied. She was so busy writing, she did not notice her mother in the doorway with a relieved smile on her careworn face.

When spring finally arrived, it seemed to Jo as if all the world had come back to life. Fiddlehead ferns poked up through the soil in the secret places in the woods where purple violets and white trillium bloomed. Jo listened to the flutelike song of the wood thrush and wondered what secrets he was singing.

With so much growing and budding and singing and winging all around her, Jo felt as if she might explode with ideas for stories. Every night she spent hunched over her desk in her writing cap, creating new exotic worlds for her characters. Sometimes she read what she wrote aloud in a grand, dramatic voice for the mice who lived in the attic.

Jo was so busy, she did not mind when Meg was invited by Aunt March to visit the Moffat family in Boston and attend countless teas, balls, and parties. What could be worse than listening to Aunt March's numerous opinions on such a long carriage ride? Jo thought.

Even before their journey began, Aunt March was busy giving Marmee advice. "I shake my head at the way you are managing Margaret," Aunt March scolded. "How is she to be married without a proper debut? Your family's only hope is for Margaret to marry well, although I don't know who marries governesses."

The trip to Boston did not improve Meg's strange behavior. When she returned, she seemed more lovesick than ever. I won't worry about Meg today, Jo told herself. I've more important things to do.

Stealthily Jo hurried to the attic, where she found her finished manuscripts. She folded and tied these with a ribbon. Then she slipped on her hat and coat. With her work safely stowed in her pocket, she slid open the rear attic window and lowered herself onto the back porch roof.

As she had done many times before, she tied her skirt around her waist and shimmied down the gutter pipe. Once she dropped into the yard, she hurried away from the house before Hannah noticed her from the kitchen window.

The merry, mysterious expression on Jo's face changed as soon as she reached Concord's dusty Main Street. As she shuffled along the boardwalk, she began to wonder. Should she go forward with her plan? Or should she give up while there was still time?

Jo walked past Hastings Dry Goods to the building with a sign that said Dentist and *The Eagle*. She took a deep breath, opened the door, and climbed the steps. To her utter amazement, it was not nearly so difficult to leave her stories as she had thought. She ran down the stairs with the editor's "Thank you, Miss March" ringing in her ears. Did that mean he would buy the stories?

Jo was so busy wondering that she did not notice that someone had fallen into step beside her.

"Hello, Mysterious," a familiar voice said, making her jump.

"Laurie! What are you doing?"

"You tell me your secret first. I saw where you went. Did you get a tooth pulled?"

Jo nodded but looked away because she knew she couldn't lie to Laurie.

"You're up to mischief, I can tell, Miss March. Tell me your secret and I'll tell you mine."

Jo began to walk even faster down the street, dodging around a horse trough, an ice wagon, and a stray dog. "Does your secret have something to do with going to Harvard in the fall?" she demanded.

"Not at all!" Laurie laughed so loudly that two women turned and looked at him in surprise.

"I know you're going to come home so brilliant, you'll find me utterly impossible to talk to or share secrets with, for that matter," Jo told him.

Laurie slowed his pace. "Nothing's going to change. I'll still be the same old Laurie. You'll still be the same old Jo."

"I wish I could go to college," she replied thoughtfully. She paused for a moment, then she gave Laurie a playful jab in the ribs. "I'll tell you my secret. Then you tell me yours." She held her hand to Laurie's ear and whispered, "I've left two stories with a newspaperman, and he's to give his answer next week."

Laurie threw his hat in the air and caught it. "Hurrah for Miss March, the famous American authoress!"

Jo blushed with delight. "Now it's your turn."

Laurie cleared his throat as they turned the corner and left Main Street. "My secret's about Meg and a certain former tutor of mine soon to be employed at the firm of Laurence and Laurence."

Jo grabbed Laurie's arm. "Liar."

Laurie put his hand to his heart and made an oath. "Has our Meg mislaid a certain personal article? Such as a glove?"

"Why, yes," Jo replied uncertainly. "She couldn't find one of her white gloves just the other day. Of course, since her trip to Boston, she's been silly as a magpie—"

"Exactly my point," Laurie said triumphantly. "I know where the glove is."

"Tell me!"

"In Mr. John Brooke's pocket. He carries it about as a romantic remembrance."

"That's horrid. I'm disgusted. I wish you hadn't told me."

"I thought you'd be pleased."

"At the idea of anybody coming to take Meg away to be married? Not at all."

"You'll feel better about it when somebody comes to take you away."

Jo stopped and looked at Laurie fiercely. "I'd like to see anyone try." Without another word, she ran as fast as she could all the way home, so fast Laurie never caught her.

Jo burst into the kitchen. She rushed to Hannah and Meg, who were rolling dough for biscuits. "Meg, I know who stole your glove. John Brooke," she said, out of breath. "He keeps it in his pocket."

To Jo's dismay, her sister blushed and actually looked pleased. "You must tell him to return it," Jo insisted. "Hannah, don't you think Mr. Brooke should give it back?"

"Isn't what I think that matters," Hannah said.

"Well, I'm going to tell Marmee," Jo announced. As she pushed open the dining room door, she heard her mother calling weakly, "Jo! Go and get your sisters." Marmee's face was pale. In her trembling hand she held a telegram for Jo to read.

MRS. MARCH:
  YOUR HUSBAND IS VERY ILL. COME AT ONCE.
                  S. HALE
                  ARMOURY SQUARE HOSPITAL
                  WASHINGTON

Seven

Jo felt as if her whole world had suddenly crashed in on her. She watched, numb, as her sobbing sisters gathered around Marmee. Jo knew that Father was much older than the other soldiers. He had never been strong or healthy. What if he was suffering and alone in that big Washington hospital, where nobody knew him, nobody cared? She clenched her fist and bit her knuckle, too overwhelmed to cry. Marmee must leave for Washington at once, before it was too late.

"The Lord keep the dear man!" Hannah said softly.

"There's no time for tears now," Marmee said

with a determined expression. "Be calm and let me think of a plan." She took out a sheet of paper and a pen from the desk. "Hannah, send a telegram saying I will come to the hospital on the next train. Jo, I want you to take this note to Aunt March and ask her politely if I might borrow money for a train ticket."

Deep in the pit of her stomach, Jo felt uneasy. What if Aunt March refused to lend the money? Jo put on her bonnet, tied the sash under her chin, and wished there were some way she could help Marmee and Father. But what could she do? Her entire savings totaled only seventy-three cents—certainly not enough for a train ticket.

"Now, Meg," Marmee said, "carry a letter to Mrs. Juba at Hope House. Mrs. King will take my place. You girls must look in on the Hummels while I'm gone. Here, Jo, now fly like the wind." Jo took the note and ran out the door.

It was nearly an hour before Jo returned. When she hurried up the sidewalk, she could already see the Laurences' carriage waiting and Marmee's carpetbag sitting nearby. She leapt up onto the porch. Before she opened the front door, she nervously tucked a wayward curl under her bonnet. She took a deep breath and opened the door.

"Where have you been?" Amy cried as soon as she saw Jo. "It's nearly seven! Marmee's ready to leave."

"Sorry," Jo said, out of breath. She bumped into John Brooke, who hurried into the hallway dressed to travel.

"Excuse me," he said, flushed with embarrassment. "I've come to offer myself as your mother's escort."

"And what are you doing?" Jo asked Laurie, who suddenly appeared in the crowded hallway, carrying a large basket.

"Our cook fixed supper for your mother," he explained. "And Grandfather sent over this bottle of spirits for your father."

Jo searched for her mother in the parlor. Marmee, already in her hat and cloak, sat at her desk writing a few more last-minute instructions. "Jo! Did Aunt March give you the money?"

Jo shook her head.

Marmee's jaw dropped in shock. Before she could speak, Jo reached into her pocket and handed her a roll of bills.

"Twenty-five dollars?" Marmee said in astonishment when she finished counting. "If this didn't come from Aunt March, where did it come from?"

Jo pulled off her bonnet. All that was left of her beautiful long hair was short, ragged stubs. "I sold my hair."

Jo's sisters gasped. "How could you?" said Amy. "It was your one beauty!"

Jo stared at her feet. "I couldn't bear to ask Aunt March for the money and listen to her tell me that it had been absurd for Father to go into the army, that she had always predicted no good would come of it, and how we should have taken her advice." She looked up and winked. "Besides I rather like my hair this way." Self-consciously she touched the back of her head. "And it will grow right back, you know."

Marmee was speechless. With tears in her eyes, she kissed Jo's forehead. Then she kissed and hugged the other girls.

"Tell Father we love him," Meg said tearfully as Marmee started toward the door.

"Tell him we pray for him," Beth said.

Amy held her mother's skirt tightly. "Don't leave me!"

"I must, Baby. Now, you do as the others tell you. And God willing, your father will soon be safe and well," Marmee said gently.

Hannah handed Marmee a loaf of bread. "I'll never forget his kindness."

Marmee gave all four girls one last hug, then whispered, "I shall miss my little women."

Late that night there was weeping upstairs from one of the girls' bedrooms. Beth awoke and sat up. She glanced over at Jo's bed, which was strangely empty. Silently she tiptoed to the old armchair where Jo sat huddled in the moonlight. Beth put her arms around her sobbing sister. "Are you thinking of Father?" she whispered.

Jo shook her shorn head. "My hair!" she cried in heartfelt misery. Beth gave her a hug, and they both began to laugh and cry at the same time.

During the first weeks that Marmee was away, Jo and her sisters tried very hard to make the best of things. But after the money ran low, they grumbled and argued over the account books. They quarreled when they had to go to bed hungry whenever it was Amy's turn to cook dinner. Only Beth seemed to know what needed to be done around the house without complaining.

"Oh, dear!" Amy said one dismal late October morning. She opened the stove and poked four blackened potatoes with a fork. Two fell on the floor and split in a brittle mess. "This stove!"

"We'll have to eat them anyway," Meg replied.

She stood in the pantry with a frustrated look on her face. "There's no cornmeal, nor coffee. The grocer won't let us have more till we pay him. We owe too much already for him to add to our account."

"What can I bring the Hummels to eat?" Beth asked.

Jo put on her cloak to go to Aunt March's. "Oh, fry the Hummels!" she said in irritation. "You spent hours there last week."

"But Marmee said—" Beth replied with worry on her face. "We can't abandon them."

Jo handed her sister two of the blackened potatoes. "Take these to them in your pockets. At least they'll keep your hands warm till you get there."

"It's not my fault I can't cook," Amy said, her lower lip quivering. "When's Marmee coming home? Seems like there's a terrible storm every day since she's been gone."

"More like an earthquake," Jo mumbled. She patted her sister's shoulder and hoped she wouldn't start crying again. "Now, chin up. I mustn't be late to work."

"Don't anyone write of our troubles to Marmee," Meg said.

"I hate money," Jo grumbled. As she headed out

On a bright Christmas Day, the sisters sang, "Love and joy come to you!"

Old Mr. Laurence and his grandson watched the strange procession.

A wonderful surprise—a letter from Father, away at the war.

By candlelight Jo wrote thrilling stories of daring and adventure.

While Beth stayed at home . . .

Jo spent hours reading to grouchy Aunt March . . .

and Amy wept, cradling the hand her teacher had rapped with his pointer.

A fragrant pear nestled inside the birdhouse post office—a gift from Laurie.

Amy's small hand splashed above the water's icy surface. "Grab hold!" Laurie called.

The best Christmas present for the Marches—Father was home!

Surrounded by friends and family, Meg and John Brooke were married.

"I love you," Laurie told Jo. "What could be more reasonable than to marry you?"

Far from home, Jo struggled with her carpetbag down the streets of New York City.

"Our subscribers aren't interested in sentiment and fairy stories," the newspaper editor told Jo.

"May I see some of your published work?" Professor
Bhaer asked.

Beth's eyes were strange and faraway, bright and feverish
with pain.

In Europe Laurie visited Amy often—and fell in love with her.

"Let us make a wonderful life together," Jo said to her beloved Friedrich. "We'll do something splendid, something that will turn the world upside down."

the door, she wondered what nasty comment Aunt March would make that day about her hair.

When Jo returned home that evening, she stopped at the birdhouse post office in the hedge. She smiled when she discovered a fragrant pear inside. Quickly she polished the sweet pear and took a bite. Laurie must be home from college for the weekend, she thought to herself. In need of funds, no doubt. We'd have a week's groceries on what he spends at billiards.

Jo leapt up the front steps two at a time and entered the house. Inside the door she spotted a letter from the postman addressed to Mr. Joseph March. "Jehosephat!" she whispered. With trembling hands, she opened the letter and let out a delighted howl.

She rushed inside waving a five-dollar note and a letter from the *Eagle*. "Amy! Beth!" she hollered. "You won't believe it. I'm an author. I just sold 'The Lost Duke of Gloucester' for five whole dollars!" Jo stomped into the kitchen. Where was everyone?

"Beth! Amy!" she called again and went into the parlor. There she found Beth slumped at the piano. Her head lay cradled in her arms as if she had fallen asleep. "Wake up!" Jo said happily. "You won't believe what I got in the mail today. Of course I got five times as much for selling a hank of hair—" She stopped when her sister lifted her head and revealed her flushed face and red-rimmed eyes. "What's wrong?"

"The Hummel baby died," Beth said sadly. She held her head with both hands. "He was so sick, poor thing. He died in my lap before his mother got home." She burst into tears.

Jo thought about the tiny baby, his tiny fingers and toes. She sniffed and wiped the corners of her eyes with her sleeve. "Beth, you don't look well. Do you feel all right?"

Beth shook her head. "My throat hurts."

"We must get you into bed right away," Jo insisted. She helped her sister upstairs and covered her with blankets. When Amy returned from the market, she promised to sit by her sister's bedside in case she needed anything. Meanwhile, Jo and Meg frantically searched Marmee's medical book to try to find some remedy for Beth's rash. "She's burning up, but she says she's freezing," Meg said. "She has a terrible thirst, but she won't drink."

Jo felt confused, hopeless. "I—I think that's arsenicum, but she looks more like belladonna."

When Hannah returned, she took off her coat

and hung it in the hallway. "It's scarlet fever," she said wearily.

"How do you know?" Jo demanded.

"I just came from the Hummels. Two children taken up to Jesus with the same illness. Where's Amy?"

"Upstairs," Jo said.

"She mustn't," Hannah said quickly. "She hasn't had scarlet fever yet the way you and Meg have."

Jo raced up the stairs and brought Amy down as fast as she could. Hannah had her cloak and satchel of clothes waiting. "We have to send you away, Baby. It's scarlet fever."

"I don't want to be sent off," Amy said in a hurt voice.

"Bless your heart," Hannah replied gently, "it's to keep you well."

"You don't want to be sick, do you?" Jo said, feeling impatient. "Laurie's coming with the carriage to take you to Aunt March's. You'll have a wonderful time."

"No, I won't," Amy said, and pouted. "Aunt March scares me. She's always cross, and she'll make me polish her silver candlesticks till my hands are ruined."

"If she's unkind, I'll send Laurie to take you

away," Jo promised. When Amy heard these words she smiled hopefully.

"Where will we go?"

"Paris, maybe," Jo said, glad to see her sister smile.

Then Amy's face grew fearful again. "If I get scarlet fever and die, give Meg my box with the green doves. Jo, you can have my most precious plaster rabbit. I'm giving Laurie the clay horse I made that he said had no neck and—"

"Be on your way now, Amy," Hannah interrupted. "I see the Laurence carriage waiting."

Amy clung to Jo. "I don't want to die," Amy said desperately. "I just thought of something else. I've never been kissed. I've waited my whole life to be kissed, and what if it never happens?"

Jo rolled her eyes. Gently she pushed Amy toward the door. "Get in the carriage now. Laurie's waiting. I need to tend to Beth." Amy gave Jo one last hug, then ran down the walk. Jo waved to Laurie and shut the door.

That night Jo and Meg took turns sitting beside Beth's bed. They wrung out cool cloths and laid them on Beth's feverish face. Her lips were parched and cracked. Her words sounded strange and fuzzy. Neither of the girls knew anything about scarlet fever. It frightened Jo when Beth spoke in a hoarse, broken voice and called her by the wrong name. Other times Beth asked for Marmee, which made Jo feel even worse because Hannah had insisted they not write to their mother to tell her of the illness.

"She can't leave Father," Meg whispered to Jo.

"Beth needs Marmee," Jo insisted. "She depends on her."

"But what if we send for her and Father gets worse? And how will we pay for the train?"

Jo frowned. In the morning she would ask Laurie what he thought they should do. She yawned. Her body ached from bending over her sister. The hours dragged by and Beth did not seem to be improving. Jo pressed a fresh cloth to her sister's forehead and tried to smooth the rumpled sheets. She will get better, she told herself, her eyes brimming with tears. She must.

The next day Beth's fever went down slightly, but by midmorning it returned. When Laurie came to the house, silent as a ghost, he brought his grandfather's doctor, Dr. Bangs. The doctor opened his satchel and took Beth's pulse. Then he listened to her breathing. He shook his head when he came into the hallway where Hannah, Meg, and Jo waited nervously. "There's nothing that can be done. It would be best to send for her mother."

Hannah nodded without speaking. Meg leaned against the wall, as if all the energy had left her. Jo stumbled trancelike downstairs and nearly fell over Laurie, who sat on the steps. She told him the grim news. "I must send a telegram as soon as possible."

"Forgive me, Jo," Laurie said, motioning for Jo to sit beside him. "I sent word yesterday. Your mother's arriving on the late train tonight."

"Tonight?" Jo gave Laurie an enormous, grateful hug.

"You're not angry?"

"Why should I be?" Jo's face clouded again when she thought of Marmee's homecoming and what terrible sadness the next hours might bring. Unashamed, she bent over and sobbed into her hands. For once she wasn't embarrassed to have someone see her cry.

Laurie put his arm around her and offered her his handkerchief. "There. There," he said gently. "I'm here."

Eight

As soon as Marmee arrived, she went right to work. She felt Beth's burning forehead and her cold hands. Then she yanked up the coverlet. Beth's feet were ice cold.

"Jo, bring a basin of vinegar and some rags. We must draw the fever down," Marmee said. "I'll need my kit, Hannah. We'll not sleep tonight."

"I'm glad you're back," Jo told her mother as she took her coat and kissed her cheek.

"And Father?" Meg whispered.

"He is doing much better, dear hearts," Marmee replied. She looked toward the hallway.

"Someone's come in. Who can be downstairs at this late hour?"

Jo followed her mother and watched her quickly descend the staircase. Marmee stopped at the bottom. Blocking the hallway was a splendid rosewood upright piano with shining brass candlestick fittings and a velvet-covered bench. Standing beside the piano was Mr. Laurence.

"Mrs. March," he said, his hat in his hand so that his silver hair seemed to glow in the candlelight. "I have brought your little daughter a gift. I know she enjoys music—" His stern voice wavered for a moment. He coughed. "The piano belonged to my little girl. She died of smallpox. I should have given it to your daughter some time ago. She's musical, isn't she?"

Marmee nodded. "Thank you, Mr. Laurence. It is most generous of you," she said, her voice trembling with emotion. "I'm sure Beth would be very happy to have it. Would you mind handing me that valise over there?

"Thank you." Marmee took the case and slowly started back up the stairs again, unaware that Jo could see her tears.

That night the entire household waited and watched. Jo sat beside the window in the parlor gazing at the moon that appeared and disappeared behind the clouds. She heard a door shut softly and someone weeping. She leapt to her feet and tiptoed up the stairs. What had happened? Hannah sat in the hallway outside Beth's room. Her strong shoulders were hunched forward as she sobbed into her apron.

Panic-stricken, Jo pushed open the door and rushed to Beth's bedside. Her mother sat beside Beth, stroking her face. Beth's eyes were open. She looked at her Mother and then at Jo. A faint smile played across her lips. "The fever's finally broken," Marmee said quietly. "Lord be praised."

Overcome with relief, Jo knelt and put her head on the bed beside Beth.

Weeks passed. Storms blew from the North Atlantic and covered Concord in snow. Letters from Washington came regularly from Mr. March, who was recovering but still too weak to travel. He wrote to his little women about the new, gleaming white Capitol building rising from the mud of Washington. He wrote with joy about "Old Abe's" election to a second term in office and how he hoped that General Grant was finally the general who would win the war for the North. In every letter, Mr. March asked about Beth and her health since the scarlet fever.

On Christmas Eve Jo sat at the parlor desk and put pen to paper:

December 1864
Christmas Eve

Dearest Father:
This is to let you know that Beth is playing piano again. Mrs. Pat-Paw and the rest of us enjoy her music. She is still weak but in her usual good spirits in spite of all. I wish you a most splendid Christmas and hope you will feel well enough to return to us soon—

Jo paused. She felt secretly sad. When would they ever be together again as they had been at long-ago Christmas holidays? She looked around the parlor. There was nothing dreary about the gathering tonight. Amy sat beside Aunt March, joking and laughing as she sorted yarn for her aunt's crewelwork with help from Laurie. Somehow even grouchy Aunt March seemed to have caught the Christmas spirit and had been very cheerful all evening.

In another corner Beth played carols at the piano while Amy and Marmee sang. Hannah shook a pan of popcorn over the stove, filling the whole house with a delicious smell. Mr. Laurence, who had become a close family friend during Beth's illness, set up a chessboard on the center table. He motioned for Jo to join him in a game.

Jo smiled. "Just a moment, Mr. Laurence. I'm almost done." She wanted to add a few more lines to describe the scene at home to Father before she sealed the letter inside the envelope.

"Grandfather," Beth called to Mr. Laurence when the carol ended. "Come here and sit by me." She patted the piano bench. "You know how absorbed Jo gets when she writes. It may be hours before she finishes that letter."

Mr. Laurence winked at Jo. "Your sister's offer might help me preserve my dignity," he said, and chuckled. "Gentlemen should always seek an honorable way to avoid defeat. Remember the last time we played chess, my dear? I think I'll let my grandson have the honors this time."

Laurie made a gallant bow and took his grandfather's place at the chessboard. "I did warn you about her, sir."

Beth handed Mr. Laurence a package wrapped in bright paper. "Merry Christmas. And thank you again for all your kindnesses."

He opened the package. "My dear child, I've never had a finer pair of slippers made for me," he said, holding her gift for everyone to see. The knit slippers were made of soft brown yarn and were lined with gray felt.

"I hope in defeat you are as gentlemanly as your grandfather," Jo teased when she sat down to play.

"Not at all," Laurie replied, narrowing his eyes.

After a good-natured round, Jo was clearly the victor.

"Just to show I've no hard feelings," Jo said, "I'll bring you coffee and a slice of cake."

She opened the kitchen door, then paused when she heard Marmee and Meg's voices. "I fear you would have a very long engagement. Three years or four," Marmee said. "We don't know how long the war will last, and John won't be mustered out until then. He has no house, his position is uncertain—"

"John?" Jo interrupted, startling her mother and sister. "Don't you mean Mr. Brooke?"

"Well, he's there at the hospital visiting Father even as we speak," Marmee said as she sliced the thick lemon cake Mr. Laurence had brought for their dessert. "And John was of invaluable assistance to me in helping your father—"

"That conniving rook!" Jo exclaimed. "Sneaking around, currying favor with the King and Queen."

"Jo!" Meg said angrily.

"To steal our girl and carry her off!" Jo clenched her fists. "Meg, I won't let him have you. Isn't that right, Marmee? We don't have to get married, do we?"

Marmee sighed and glanced at Meg with a tender look of concern. "Better never to be married than be unhappy."

Meg's face flushed. "Do you think," she said indignantly, "that I would be unhappy married to John?"

"Poky old Brooke?" Jo rubbed her hands together. "He's dull as powder and poor besides."

"Jo," Marmee scolded gently, "I'd rather Meg be a poor man's wife and well loved, than marry for riches and lose her self-respect."

"Then you don't mind that John Brooke is poor?" Meg asked, her voice full of hope.

"Well, I should like John to be established in a good business first," Marmee replied uncertainly.

Jo puffed up her cheeks in disgust. "You're not going to let her get married, are you?"

"It's a proposal, nothing more. It needn't be decided right now," Marmee said.

Jo did not feel the least bit reassured. It seemed dismally clear that everything had already been decided. Meg was going to marry John Brooke and nothing between Meg and her sisters would ever be the same—not the Pickwick Society, the plays, or the secrets. Suddenly an even more disturbing thought entered Jo's head. If Meg gave up her freedom so easily for marriage, did everyone expect Jo to do the same?

Well, I won't! Jo said to herself. She sloshed coffee from the cup onto the cake as she bumped open the dining room door with one hip.

A cold blast of air came through the house. Excited voices drifted from the hallway. The front door slammed shut. Jo thumped the coffee and cake on the table to see who had come in.

"Another Christmas present for the March family!" announced the unmistakable voice of John Brooke.

Not him, Jo thought, disappointed. As she came into the hallway, she noticed someone else. A thin, stooped figure in a faded Union chaplain's uniform. "Father!" she cried excitedly, and ran to him.

Mr. March embraced her awkwardly with his one good arm. The other was bound in a splint and hung stiffly at his side. Jo's sisters surrounded their father with shouts of joy. He looked tired but happy as he hugged each one. Briskly he wiped his eyes with a handkerchief. "Let me see you all. Jo, your hair might become the fashion."

Jo blushed, pleased.

"We've waited forever and ever," Amy said.

Beth gave Mr. March another hug. "You're the best Christmas present of all!"

"You grew a beard!" Meg exclaimed, and kissed her father on the cheek.

Beth smiled. "I think he looks very handsome."

"I think he looks very puny," said Aunt March. Her shrill voice shook with emotion as she rose from her chair. "Welcome home, nephew."

"It is good to be home," Mr. March said. "Merry Christmas!"

"Come and rest." Marmee ushered her husband to the couch for him to sit down. "Amy, get your father some coffee and cake. Meg, take his cloak. Help him with his boots, Jo."

"Now, now," Mr. March protested, his eyes twinkling. "I'm not used to so much attention. Don't coddle this old soldier."

"We'll coddle you until you're completely well again," Marmee replied. She held her husband's good hand with great tenderness.

"Well, I hope your coddling works," Mr. March replied with a fond glance at Marmee and then at John Brooke and Meg, "for I mean to dance at our daughter's wedding."

Meg blushed. John Brooke made a stiff, formal bow. Jo abruptly left the room and hurried up to the attic. For several moments, she sat in the darkness and rested with her forehead on her knees until her breathing sounded normal again.

"Jo?" Laurie's voice called. He tiptoed up the steps and sat beside her. "Isn't it wonderful about Meg and John?" he asked eagerly.

"Yes, wonderful," Jo replied, glad that he could not see her face and realize that she was lying.

Nine

*N*early three years passed before Meg and John Brooke were married in the Laurences' garden. In the bright sunlight of April 1867, surrounded by friends and family, Jo was nearly able to convince herself that the war had been nothing more than a half-forgotten, terrible nightmare. Purple lilacs had begun to bud. Redbud blossomed, and pale pink cherry blossoms filled the air with fragrance.

The only reminders of the war were the uniforms worn by a few former officers who attended the ceremony. Their brass buttons gleamed, and their boots shone. A few wore black armbands above their elbows in memory of their commander-in-chief, President Abraham Lincoln, who had been killed by an assassin's bullet two years earlier in April, the same month the war ended.

Father conducted the wedding ceremony in his quiet, earnest manner. He stood before Meg and John, who held hands. Meg looked beautiful in her simple white dress, with lilies of the valley in her bodice and her hair—certainly not the fancy wedding outfit she had bragged about years earlier. John was not a rich man. His job as a bookkeeper in Concord had provided him with just enough money to buy a small, modest house for his bride. But they both looked happy and filled with hope as the wedding guests sang, " 'For the beauty of the earth, for the glory of the skies, for the love which from our birth, over and around us lies . . .' "

As they sang, Jo shot a glance at Amy. Just sixteen, she had blossomed into an uncommonly pretty young woman. Beth smiled at Jo and squeezed her hand three times in their secret message that meant, "I love you." Jo returned the message and grinned at her sister. Beth's gaunt face and dark-circled eyes remained haunting reminders of her continuing battles with illness.

Jo looked across the crowd at Laurie. He appeared handsome and grown up in his formal afternoon coat. His hair was combed back, and he had grown a mustache, as was the fashion in college. He seemed to be watching her carefully over the top of his hymnbook in a way that made her feel very uncomfortable. She pretended she did not notice and was glad when the service ended and she could escape.

Jo dodged between wedding guests nibbling cake and drinking last fall's cider. She hurried away from the garden, even though she knew there was no real reason to flee so secretly. Nobody was paying any attention to her. All eyes were on the radiant bride and groom.

When she found a shady spot beneath a large oak, she sat down. She leaned against the rough bark and removed her uncomfortable feathered hat. The day's festivities had made her feel even more restless, confused, and irritable than ever. She rubbed her foot and thought about how fine it would be to take off her tight boots and run barefoot in the long grass. But she knew she couldn't. The yard was crammed with company. What would their guests think? Jo sighed. Was every place as boring and dull as Concord? There must be somewhere in the world where people exchanged brilliant ideas, a place where there were other topics of conversation besides spring rain and cow manure and the price of flour.

"You've been avoiding me," Laurie said, startling her.

Jo tried to recover her composure. "No, I'm not. How is the conquering graduate? I'm sure your grandfather must be so proud you've finished at Harvard."

Laurie plucked a piece of grass and put it in his mouth. He sat down beside Jo. "Yes, and exceedingly bent on locking me up in one of his offices. Why is it that Amy may paint pictures on china plates and you may scribble stories, while I must manfully set my music aside?"

"Pardon me!" Jo replied hotly. "I work at my scribbles. My family puts to good use the money I earn selling my stories. And if Amy paints china, it's only because china is what a lady paints. Any broader ambition would be called masculine. But if you wish to study music—"

"I'd have to defy Grandfather."

"Yes, but not the whole of society."

Laurie lay on his back, his hands behind his head, gazing up at the clouds. "I can't go against the old man." He rolled over on his side when Jo tickled his neck with a dandelion. He looked at her tenderly. "When I imagine myself in the life of a gentleman that Grandfather has planned for me, I can think of only one thing that would make me happy."

Jo tossed the dandelion. "Oh, Laurie, don't."

"I have loved you since the moment I clapped eyes on you. What could be more reasonable than to marry you?"

Jo sighed. "We'd kill each other."

"Nonsense."

"Neither of us can keep our temper."

"I can, unless provoked."

"We're both stupidly stubborn, especially you. We'd only quarrel."

"I wouldn't."

"You can't even propose without quarreling."

Laurie laughed as if he agreed with the truth of what she said. He sat up and put his arm around her. "Jo, dear Jo, I swear I'd be a saint. I'd let you win every argument. And I'd take care of you and your family and give you every luxury you've ever been denied, and you won't have to scribble at your little stories."

Jo broke free from his embrace. "But I don't want to stop writing."

"Well, don't stop, if it amuses you."

Jo frowned. Why couldn't he understand that writing was like breathing to her? It was something she simply *had* to do.

"Grandfather will give us his house in London," Laurie continued in his most charming manner. "He wants me to learn the business there. Can't you see us larking around London? You'll hardly have time to write."

Jo plucked another dandelion and twirled the stem between her palms. "I'm not fashionable enough for London. You need someone elegant and refined."

"I want you."

Jo looked away. "Please don't ask me."

Laurie jumped to his feet and began to angrily brush pieces of grass from his fine suit. His hurt expression made Jo feel worse than ever. "I am so desperately sorry," she said in a quiet voice. "I do care for you, with all my heart. But I can't go and be a wife. It's everything I've never wanted."

Laurie stared down at her in anger. "You say you won't, but you will. There'll come a time when you'll meet some man—a good man—and you'll love him tremendously and live and die for him. You will, Jo, I know you. And I'll be hanged if I stand by and watch." Laurie stomped away, leaving Jo alone.

It took several moments for her to realize exactly what she had just done. Her hands shook as she tried to smooth her rumpled bonnet. She stood slowly and walked back toward the wedding celebration. As she did, she glanced at the hedge between her house and the Laurences'.

The little birdhouse post office was gone.

A few days later, Beth helped Jo pack her books from the attic into a trunk. They did not speak. Jo's eyes were red from crying.

"Are you ill?" Amy asked Jo from the attic stairway.

Jo turned brusquely away. "She has refused Laurie," Beth explained.

"I'm sure she can take it back," Amy said, stunned. "It's just a misunderstanding."

Jo shook her head. "No." Amy still looked as if she did not understand.

"No," Beth said in a soft echo.

"I must go away," Jo said with determination.

Amy spoke up. "Aunt March is going to France."

"France!" Jo said, suddenly brightening. She

had always wanted to go to Europe. Now at last she'd have her chance. Maybe everything would work out just fine after all. Maybe—

"Jo," Amy said, interrupting her thoughts. "Aunt March has asked me to go."

At first Jo could not speak. "To Europe? To *my* Europe?"

"Well, I am Aunt March's companion now," Amy said with a touch of pride. "It's a good opportunity. I am to study painting. And Aunt March hopes that with a little polish I shall make a good match abroad."

"Oh," said Jo. She shut the trunk and sat down as if all the air had just been knocked out of her.

That evening Jo cried with her face buried in Marmee's lap. "I'm going to New York," she said fiercely between sobs. "I'll stay with your friend Mrs. Kirke. You said her daughters needed a tutor. I'll see the world. I'll write. Maybe I'll be published. You needn't worry about me."

Marmee gently stroked Jo's hair. "It isn't easy for little birds to leave the nest. And just as hard for me to let you go. Amy found a way to try her wings. And you must go, too, though I don't know what I'll do without my Jo. I pray you'll find your happiness. Go and have your liberty and see what comes of it."

Ten

New York City was the farthest from home Jo had ever traveled by herself. She felt confident until the engine pulled into the enormous depot and she stepped out of the train car. Immediately she was swallowed up in a river of pushing, shoving people—more people than she'd seen before in one place in her life.

She struggled with her carpetbag down narrow, crowded streets where the stores and houses were so squeezed together, she could hardly see the sky. From windows hung ragged clothes, dirty bedding, lines of laundry. On wider streets the buildings loomed at either side like mountains—five, six stories.

The street noise was deafening. Peddlers shouted from carts filled with cabbage, fresh fish, apples, chickens still squawking in crates. So many different people, she did not understand their words. What language were they speaking? A scissor grinder called for customers. An organ grinder's music played, drowned out by the sounds of horse hooves on cobblestones and steel wheel rims biting against gravel and pavement.

A mob of pale-faced children screamed and scrambled in the gutter, flipping pennies. Stray dogs barked. The streets smelled of every smell imaginable—manure, baked potatoes, smoke, dust, leather, human sweat, and stinking garbage from overturned cans and alley heaps.

Whenever Jo paused to read the scrap of paper with directions to Mrs. Kirke's building, someone knocked into her and pushed her along. There was no place to stop, no place to rest. Her feet ached. Her stomach growled. Where was Eleven Waverly Place? Every sign confused her. What would happen if night came and she still did not find the right address? Where would she sleep? The city was not safe, Hannah had warned her. Nobody would help her. They would only rob her—or worse.

Jo held her carpetbag tightly against herself. "Hey, beautiful!" a group of men shouted at her, and whistled as she walked past. They were dark and leering, and she felt afraid but kept walking, more quickly now.

She turned the corner. Waverly Place! She followed the numbers on the tall brick buildings until at last she found the brownstone building that matched the address on the paper. She looked up and felt afraid. The place seemed much larger and more imposing than she had expected. She looked down at her muddy skirt and touched her hair, which hung in limp strands about her facc. She must look a sight. What would Mrs. Kirke think of her?

Timidly Jo knocked on the door. No one answered. For a moment she considered running away, back to Concord, while she still had a chance. But she had no money left. She should never have left home, she told herself. She should never have come to New York at all.

Suddenly the door swung open. "You must be Josephine March, the new tutor," a short, stout woman with a friendly smile announced. She wore an apron over her linen dress. "Come in, my dear. I'm Mrs. Kirke. I'll show you your room. Follow me."

Jo struggled with her carpetbag up three flights of stairs. She was jostled by three young men, who also appeared to be boarders in Mrs. Kirke's building. They clomped past and tipped their hats. "I'm sorry I'm late," Jo said, out of breath. Where was her room? What if she collapsed before she found it?

"I hope you'll like your room. It's all I have left," Mrs. Kirke said. She took a key from a large ring that hung at her side and opened a door. The funny little sky parlor was dark and airless. Jo walked in and turned around. The room was so small, there was barely space for an iron cot, a table, chair, and small stove.

Mrs. Kirke drew open the dusty, torn curtains. "It's a fine view," she said, pointing to the church steeple below. "You won't spend all your time up here, my dear. The nursery where you are to teach and sew is a very pleasant room next to my private parlor. You'll take your meals with all the others in the dining room downstairs."

Jo nodded. She felt oddly happy. This room was to be *hers.* For once she did not have to share a bedroom with anyone. She could stay up as late as she wished writing thrilling tales and no one would complain and tell her to go to sleep. She looked around again and decided the shabby room and everything about it was absolutely perfect.

"Now leave your bags here, my dear," Mrs. Kirke said. "I'd like you to come downstairs and meet my daughters. The nursery's on the second floor, third door on the right. I just heard the tea bell. I must run and change my cap."

When Mrs. Kirke left, Jo removed her coat. She glanced in the cracked mirror on the wall and tried to smooth her rumpled hair. To make herself look more presentable, she slipped on a clean skirt, the only other one she had brought along.

She hurried down the steps. Her stomach began to jump. She didn't even know the little girls' names. What if they hated her? Jo turned a doorknob. Nothing happened. Wrong door. She moved to the next and paused.

What had Mrs. Kirke said? Second door on the third floor? Or third door on the second floor? There were so many doors in the long hallway, she did not know which one to try. She opened another. Inside, a startled-looking fat man was smoking a pipe. "Sorry," Jo said, her face flushed with embarrassment. She shut the door.

Two doors were locked. Three more led to dark

rooms. Jo sighed. She did not know where Mrs. Kirke had gone. Even if she managed to find her employer, what would happen if she asked where the children were? She'd seem so irresponsible, she would probably be fired.

When Jo had almost given up hope, she pushed open one last door. She heard a terrible roar. A man with wavy brown hair tumbled all over his head was crawling on his hands and knees on the floor. Riding on his back was a little girl about eight years old. Another little girl, with black braids, who seemed to be perhaps six, led the man about the room with a jump rope attached to his collar.

"Ephulant! Ephulant! Faster, faster!" the girls shouted. The beast with wire-rim glasses lumbered between two overturned chairs.

Jo stood speechless and watched as the little girls screamed with delighted laughter. "Hello," she finally said, announcing her presence.

The man looked up. His ruddy face blushed. He slipped his rider from her perch and jumped to his feet. *"Ach!* I am so sorry," he said with a German accent. He held out a big hand in welcome. "We did not see you come in. I am Professor Friedrich Bhaer. You must be the new tutor?"

Jo nodded. She was surprised by how strong and warm his hand felt. The professor seemed a gentleman, although two buttons were off his worn coat and there was a patch on one of his shoes. "I am just arrived from Concord today," she said. "Mrs. Kirke said I should begin my new job as soon as possible."

"Of course, of course," he said. The little girls danced around him, intent on continuing the game of elephant. "This is Minnie and this is Kitty." The girls darted back and forth around the chairs in a game of tag.

"Tell us stories, Mr. Bear!" demanded the blond one called Minnie. "About the storks stuck in the chimney."

"No!" Kitty insisted. "The one about the fairies who ride snowflakes out of the sky."

The professor smiled and shook his head. "This is your new tutor, Miss March. She will be teaching you reading and arithmetic lessons, my little *kinder*."

The little girls groaned. Clearly they preferred elephants, storks, and fairies to reading and arithmetic. Jo tried to smile encouragingly. "I know a story called 'The Seven Bad Pigs,'" she said. "Would you like to hear it?"

"Now!" Kitty and Minnie said. They tugged Jo's skirt and pulled her toward the sofa to begin the tale.

"I will be going, Miss March," the professor said, and slipped toward the doorway. He made a formal bow. "If I hear these naughty ones go to vex you, Miss March, call at me and I come." He made a threatening frown at the little girls, who only laughed.

Jo soon discovered that Mrs. Kirke was a demanding boss. She required Jo to watch the girls from very early in the morning until they finally were ready to go to sleep. Even so, Jo found time to write many letters home to her family. She often asked about Beth's health and of Amy, who was still away in Europe.

Every night Jo worked late writing thrilling tales featuring dead bodies, poisonous snakes, and escaped convicts—all the sensational kinds of stories that she discovered New York newspapers would buy for twenty-five or thirty dollars on publication. "The more bizarre the better," the editor from the *Weekly Volcano* told her.

The money seemed so wonderful that Jo wrote more and more. There were so many marvelous things she could think of doing with the money—a trip to the seashore for Beth, a new dress for Marmee, books for Father.

When she wasn't writing, her mind was churning with new story ideas. While out on the streets taking Kitty and Minnie to the park, Jo studied and memorized faces of the most unusual-looking passersby to use in her tales. Whenever she could, she went to the library with the girls. While they were busy reading fairy stories, Jo secretly examined works on poisons and weaponry.

She did not have much social life. She felt shy and awkward when she ate her meals with the other boarders at the long table in Mrs. Kirke's dining room. She often finished quickly to avoid having to speak to anyone. But one evening she saw an elderly woman with a kind face at the end of the table. Jo took a seat beside her. Sitting at the other end of the table was Professor Bhaer, who shouted answers to a deaf old gentleman while he ate his soup.

Jo kept her gaze down as she ate the tough beef and boiled potatoes. A few seats away she overheard two young men speaking to each other as they shot glances in her direction.

"Who's the new party?"

"Governess or something of that sort."

"What the deuce is she at our end of the table for?"

"Friend of the old lady's."

"Handsome head but no style."

Jo bristled with anger. She did not like being discussed as if she were a piece of furniture. She was glad when the two men got up and left the table to smoke in the parlor. Because she did not want to pass them in the hallway, she stayed at the table longer than she usually did. To waste time, she chased the last of her cold, slimy lima beans around her plate with her fork.

When the last diners rose from the table and left, only the professor remained. He stood up and gestured in a friendly way for her to come and join him. Jo felt embarrassed but did not wish to be insulting and did as he requested.

Ceremoniously, he went to the sideboard and found two clean coffee cups. He placed them on the table, put two cubes of sugar in each, and filled them with coffee. "When first I saw you, I thought, Ah, she is a writer."

Jo blushed. "What made you think so?"

The professor offered her coffee, then pointed to the middle finger and forefinger on her right hand.

Her fingers were stained with ink. "I know many writers. In Heidelberg I was a professor at the university," he said, and laughed cheerfully. "Here I am only a man with an accent. You are far from home, too, Miss March? You miss your family?"

Jo nodded, suddenly overwhelmed by homesickness. "Very much," she admitted. "And you, do you miss your wife and family, too?"

"I have no wife," the professor replied.

Jo cleared her throat, worried that she had been too bold asking such a personal question. "Europe has always sounded like such a wonderful place. I have hoped to go there and see all the sights."

The professor chuckled. "I can see you have much energy. I like that. The world is a very big, very wonderful place. May I ask to see some of your work?"

"My published work?" Jo said, pleased by his attention. She hadn't shown her latest stories to anyone, not even her family.

"You are published? *Das is gut!* I *am* impressed."

Jo slipped out the newspaper she had bought that afternoon from a newsboy. Shyly, she pushed the *Weekly Volcano* across the table and pointed to the second page.

He adjusted his spectacles. "I do not know this paper. Ah. 'The Sinner's Corpse,' by Joseph March. You use another name?" As he began reading, his expression changed. "They pay well, I suppose," he said when he finished. He did not look pleased.

Jo felt crushed. She jutted out her jaw defensively. "People's lives are dull. They want thrilling stories."

"People want whiskey, but I think you and I do not care to sell it." He pointed to the page. "This is a waste of your mind. Lunatics, vampires—"

"You may think what you wish," Jo said angrily, "but my stories help my family buy the things they need." She pushed herself away from the table and stood up. She blinked back tears, embarrassed that someone might come into the dining room and see her so upset.

"Please," the professor said softly, "I do not wish to insult you. Understand me. I am saying, you must please yourself. You must write about what you know, about what is important to you. I can see you have talent."

"You can?"

"Yes, but you should be writing something from your life, from the depths of your soul. There is more in you than this," he said, pointing to the newspaper, "if you have the courage to write it."

Jo tried to feel hopeful and encouraged by his comment, but she only felt confused. What was there about her life that was worth writing about? Slowly she folded the newspaper.

"Do not seem discouraged by this professor's words," he said, and smiled. "I make a humble gift. An experience. Do you like the opera? *Faust* is playing tonight."

Jo looked at him, speechless. She had never been to an opera before. "I don't have an opera dress."

"You are perfect. Where we are sitting, we will not be so formal." Professor Bhaer stood and gestured toward the door. Grandly he held her cloak for her.

That evening the stage manager, who was a friend of Professor Bhaer's, ushered them up a ladder backstage to a perch high above the stage. At first Jo felt frightened by the dizzying height. But she was soon swept away by the opera's enchanting music and dramatic story, which the professor quietly translated for her from the French. So engrossed was Jo that she did not notice the stagehands hauling ropes and lugging scenery backstage. She saw only the two lovers on stage. When she stole a glance at Professor Bhaer, she was surprised that he was not watching the performance. He was watching her. Jo blushed and felt oddly startled and pleased.

Eleven

～

Jo enjoyed the professor's company on trips to art galleries and museums with the little girls. She was pleased when he offered to teach her German and Shakespeare if she would darn his socks and mend his shabby clothes. In his splendid booming voice he read aloud to her from German fairy tales and, like a big bumble bee, sang German folk songs. Then he would turn Mrs. Kirke's hyacinth bulbs toward the sun and pet Minnie and Kitty's striped cats, who received him like an old friend.

The professor was unlike anyone Jo had ever known. One evening in spring, Jo sat at her small table in her room and gazed out the window as she wrote a letter home to her family. As she had so many times before in her letters, she tried to describe Professor Bhaer. "He is very learned and gives lessons to support himself," she wrote to her mother. "He is neither rich, great, young, nor handsome, but he has the kindest eyes I ever saw—"

There was a knock at the door. "Telegram, Josephine!"

Jo opened the door. "Thank you, Mrs. Kirke." Nervously she slit open the envelope and read the words. She slumped onto the chair.

"Serious?" Mrs. Kirke asked with concern.

Jo nodded. "I must go home at once," Jo said slowly. "It's my sister Beth."

As soon as Jo arrived home, she hurried up to Beth's room. She was surprised and shocked by what she saw. Her sister's cheeks were sunken and colorless. Her hands lay thin and bony upon the quilt. For several moments Jo watched Beth sleep. Her sister's pale lips moved, her forehead creased as if in pain. She coughed. Jo touched her sister's brow tenderly. Still, Beth did not wake.

Jo sank onto the edge of the bed. She felt as if she had been betrayed. "Why did you wait so long to telegraph?" she whispered to her mother when she came into the room.

Marmee sighed. She looked much older and more exhausted with worry than Jo had remembered. "Beth would not let us send for you sooner," Marmee said, and took out a handkerchief. "We have had Dr. Bangs in so many times. But it is beyond all of us now. Dear Beth is worn out with the coughing and the pain. She doesn't eat. She sleeps fitfully. I don't know how she has held on."

Jo put her arm around her mother, who began to cry softly. Everything seemed so unreal now that she was home again. There were Beth's mending basket, her beloved dolls, and her fine rosewood piano, just as they had been before Jo left. Outside the sun shown. The sky was bright blue. A gentle May breeze moved the white curtains and filled the bedroom with the scent of lilacs that grew beside the house. How could everything be blooming and full of life outdoors, when here inside the house her sister struggled for every breath?

Early that evening Beth finally opened her eyes. Jo sat beside her sister's bed and offered her a cup of hot broth. Beth, propped up with many pillows, gazed fondly at Jo. But her eyes were strange and faraway, bright and feverish with pain.

On the table beside the bed stood a candle, a small blue bottle, and a glass of water with a spoon. "You're going to drink all of this good broth and you're going to get better," Jo said, smiling confidentially. "Here comes Mrs. Pat-Paw prowling under your bed. She insists you get better, too."

With great effort, Beth reached out her fragile hand to beckon to the cat. "She won't come to me. Bad cat," she whispered, then turned to Jo. "I'm glad you're home, Jo. I feel stronger with you close by. Do you know how much I've missed you?"

"And I've missed you, too," Jo said, and bit her lip. She turned away so that her sister could not see her eyes. "You drink all this broth and I'll do my man-with-a-cigar imitation. I bet that would make you feel better." Jo tried very hard to smile convincingly, but she could not help feeling guilty. She should never have gone away and left her sister.

Tenderly she lifted Beth's head so that she could sip the broth. "You're going to be fine. Don't worry. Everything's going to be all right."

Beth took only one sip, then leaned back, as if exhausted. "If God wants me with him, there is none who will stop him."

"Don't talk like that."

"Death doesn't frighten me. I've thought about it a lot," Beth said quietly. "I was never like the rest of you. Making plans about the great things I'd do. I never saw myself as anything much. Not a great writer like you."

Jo put the cup of broth on the table. "Oh, Beth. I am not a great writer."

"One day you will be." Beth glanced around the room. "Why does everyone want to go away? I love being home. But I don't like being left behind. Now I am the one going ahead."

"Beth, you're not going anywhere. You're staying right here with me."

Beth coughed. "I'm not afraid," she said in a reassuring voice. "I can be brave like you. The only hard part now is leaving you all. I know that I shall be homesick for you, even in heaven."

Jo took her sister's hand and held it tightly. She fought back tears. "I will not let you go."

Suddenly Mrs. Pat-Paw darted out from under the bed. The cat's back arched. It gazed at the window, which had been closed tight against the night air.

"What is it, Mrs. Pat-Paw?" Jo asked. The wind moaned and rattled the pane. Everything in the room seemed to vibrate strangely. The cat purred a low, strange noise. Jo gulped. She stood up to go to the window and open it. As soon as she lifted the window, the cat jumped to the sill, leapt into a tree branch, and disappeared. Jo closed the window and locked it.

When she turned to Beth, her sister looked as if she had just fallen peacefully asleep. Her hand was tucked under her cheek. When Jo came closer, she realized her sister was past sleep, past dreaming. Jo froze. She waited to see her sister's shoulders rise and fall, for her to begin breathing again.

Nothing happened.

Jo took a step forward. She picked up Beth's delicate hand, light now as a bird's wing, and began to cry very softly.

On the day of Beth's funeral, a telegram came from France. Marmee stood in the parlor, dressed in black. The mirrors were covered, the clock had been stopped, the window shades were drawn, as was the custom when someone died. Father gazed numbly into the unlit grate of the stove. Jo sat in a stiff-backed chair.

"Aunt March is bedridden, and her rheumatism forbids a sea voyage," Marmee said, folding the telegram. "Amy must bide her time and come home later. I know Laurie will go to Switzerland to console her if he can."

"Laurie is in Switzerland?" Jo asked. Laurie. He always knew how to cheer her up. For the first time in ever so long, she missed his company.

"Amy told us in letters he visits often."

"Often?" Jo said, taken aback. She had never thought of her sister Amy and Laurie as sweethearts. To her surprise, she did not feel jealous. Jo's feelings for Laurie had not changed. She was glad that her sister and Laurie might be happy together.

What bothered Jo was something else. A strange, sad sense that her family would never be the same. Everything had changed. Beth was gone from them forever. No one knew when Amy would return. Jo sat in silence for several moments, then asked quietly of her parents, as if the sorrow was too great to bear alone, "Will we ever be together again?"

Neither Marmee nor Father answered.

For days Jo felt as if she were living like a ghost. She felt nothing, said nothing. She had no appetite. She could not sleep at night. The only place she could escape the terrible sadness that filled the house was the woods. As she ran along a path, she yanked open the button of her high black collar and shook her hair free. She ran as if she could escape from Beth's death. Her heart pounded in her ears. She gulped for air. Faster and faster she sped, hurdling fallen branches and the narrow stream. When she reached the edge of the woods, she slowed to a walk. Bitterness lingered on her tongue. She felt numb with exhaustion, all hope gone.

She leaned against a great oak. Looking up into the budding leaves she heard the song of warblers. From nearby underbrush came the sound of a cricket.

Cricket, the pet name Marmee had given Beth.

Jo bent over and sobbed when she thought of her sister, the only one she could count on to listen to her troubles, schemes, and grand plans. Who would listen to her now that Beth was gone?

Jo wiped her face with her sleeve. Perhaps she knew what to do after all.

She ran across the meadow toward home. When she reached the back door, she entered silently, greeting no one. She hurried to the attic, a place she had not visited in nearly six months. How dusty and neglected the little room seemed.

Jo opened the tin box. There was still plenty of paper, a pen, a bottle of ink. She cleared the table. When she placed two hatboxes on the floor, she noticed a simple trunk painted in childish letters:

Beth. Carefully she opened the trunk and discovered two of Beth's old dolls, five old copies of the *Pickwick Portfolio,* and the paper badge that said P.S. that had once belonged to Mr. Tupman of the Pickwick Society. Jo fingered the badge and turned ever so slowly, half expecting to see all her sisters gathered at the table once again.

She placed the doll in one of the chairs and took another seat. There was still someone in whom she could confide, someone who would listen to everything that had happened, everything that was important to her. She smiled and picked up the pen and began writing.

The story that unfolded in page after page was about Jo's family, the people she knew best. She wrote of Meg's complaints on Christmas during the war and the day Beth received the new piano. She wrote about how Amy left school because of twenty-four limes and what happened when she had her own thick hair shorn from her head.

There was nothing romantic or exotic about what she described. The scenes she recalled filled her with great warmth and great sadness. She was transported to a different place, a different time, when they had all been together—Meg, Jo, Beth, and Amy.

The manuscript took several days to finish. And

when she knew it was done, she stared at the thick stack of paper for a long time before she thought what to do next. Inspired, she slipped the manuscript into a large brown envelope. In large clear print she wrote on the front: Professor Friedrich Bhaer, 11 Waverly Place, New York, New York.

Twelve

Months passed. The elms, locusts, and maples in Concord turned deep yellow and crimson. Cold winds from the northeast returned once more. On a bright October morning, laundry billowed on the line at the March house. Row upon row of white diapers flapped in the breeze. Hannah and John Brooke picked winter squash from the garden. Inside the house, in the kitchen, Meg stooped over a washtub, carefully pouring water from a kettle to wash wriggling Demi, her baby son. He and his twin sister, Daisy, had been born four weeks earlier—much to the delight of the entire March family.

Jo, her face covered with flour, stood at the counter kneading soft white bread dough. As she worked, she used the toe of her boot to rock the cradle that held Daisy. Every so often Jo absentmindedly gazed out the window. The laundry seemed to dance in the wind as restlessly as her own spirit.

It wasn't as if Jo had been unhappy staying at home to help her sister with her twin babies. The fact was that she secretly felt lonely. When she least expected it, an old feeling came again—not bitter as it once was, but a sorrowfully patient wonder. Why should Meg and Amy have all they asked for and she have nothing?

"A penny for your thoughts," Meg said as she dried Demi with a thick towel.

Jo shrugged. "I was thinking about the past, I guess. Where I've been, where I'm going."

"What happened to your friend, the German professor from New York? You know who I mean, don't you?" When Jo gave her sister a baffled look, Meg laughed. "You always wrote such long letters to us about him. I fancied that you two discussed more than books and opera."

"However did you think that?" Jo said, kneading the dough and rocking the baby more briskly.

"I'm a failure at romance, I fear. I sent him something and he did not respond."

Meg dressed the baby in a clean shirt. "But if he did respond, and you could mend your friendship as you say, would you?"

Jo paused and looked out the window into the garden. "Sometimes I wish I had someone to love as you love John. But now that I'm nearly twenty-three, I don't think I'll ever get married."

Meg laughed. "Oh, Jo. You might surprise yourself."

The front gate bell jingled. Jo glanced at her floury hands and dress with dismay. "Whoever can that be?"

She hurried to the front door and to her surprise, there stood Laurie grinning broadly. "You are absolutely covered with flour!" he explained.

Jo, speechless, gave him an affectionate hug. "Now you are, too. Stand back and let me look at you. Europe agreed with you."

"Dear Jo, you are glad to see me, then?"

Jo nodded.

Laurie smiled and looked to the right and left to see if anyone might be coming. "I'm so glad I caught you alone because there's something I want to tell you," he said sheepishly. "Six weeks ago Amy and I were married in Paris."

"Mercy on us!" Jo said, and waved a floury towel in mock horror. "What dreadful thing will you do next, ridiculous boy?"

"Jo, you're not surprised. You're no good at fooling me. Who told you?"

"I have secret spies all over Europe." Jo laughed and gave him an affectionate hug. "Actually, Aunt March wrote to us two weeks ago. I'm delighted. Congratulations to you both. But where are Amy and Aunt March?"

"Amy's coming slowly up the road with Grandfather to give me time to break the news to your family. As for Aunt March, she's confined to bed at Plumfield. Now tell me truthfully. Don't I look like a married man and the head of a family?"

Jo smiled. "Not a bit and you never will. You're the same old scapegrace as ever. Why didn't you tell us earlier yourself?"

"We wanted to surprise you," Laurie said, and cleared his throat. "Jo dear, I want to say one thing before the others come. Then we'll put it by forever. I still love you, will you believe it? Can't we go back to the happy old times when we first knew one another?"

"I'll believe it with all my heart, but we can never be boy and girl again," Jo said slowly. "We're both grown up. The happy old times can't come back, and we mustn't expect it." She smiled at him. "Don't look so sad. We'll always be friends. Now come inside and tell the others the good news." She took Laurie's hand and led him inside.

That evening, for the first time in ever so long, the family was gathered together. The noisy parlor was crowded with howling babies and talkative grown-ups—Amy and Laurie; Meg and her husband, John; Mr. Laurence; Marmee and Father, still dressed in mourning black. Jo looked about the room, listening to snatches of chatter. The only seat that was empty was the piano bench, Beth's spot. Jo sat down and placed her hand softly on the keys. She looked up in surprise when Amy joined her.

"You must tell me the truth, as my sister," Amy said in a low voice. "Do you mind at all about Laurie and me?"

"I'll admit I was surprised at first," Jo said. She laughed. So did Amy. Laurie looked up from the chessboard. Jo signaled for him to join them. "At last we're all family, as we should have been," Jo said, and kissed her sister fondly. "Now, Laurie, tell me that you and Amy will always live close by. I could not bear losing another sister."

Thirteen

∽

*I*t came as a complete surprise to Jo when she received word that Aunt March had left her entire estate in her care after she died, in January 1869. Jo, Marmee, and Amy went to the old house, which was dusty and empty—nothing like the spotless, fussy place Jo remembered.

Jo pulled a cloth from a mirror. Behind her she saw her mother and Amy wandering through the echoing formal dining room. "Jo, what will you do with so many dishes?" Amy asked as she opened a dining room cabinet filled with hundreds of pieces of china.

"It will be very costly just to heat this place,"

Marmee said, holding Aunt March's poodle. "What could Aunt March have been thinking?"

Jo walked along the bookcase touching the leather-bound volumes she loved so well. "Most likely she felt sorry for me. A homeless spinster," she said, trying to make a joke. "Poor Aunt. Imagine living here all those years by herself."

Marmee walked into the biggest parlor and parted the long heavy curtains. "People with money never seem to know how to use it. Wouldn't Plumfield make a wonderful school?"

Jo looked about, suddenly inspired. "A school."

"What a great undertaking that would be," Marmee said.

Jo pulled the curtains closed and felt a twinge of sadness. "Too great for one person."

One evening in late March, the first heavy rains of spring came. Jo hurried home from the market with her umbrella. To save time she clambered over the garden wall and hurried up the steps of the back porch to the kitchen. "Hello!" she said to Aunt March's skittery poodle, which ran to greet her, barking and dancing around her feet. Jo dumped wet parcels on the counter and began to yank off her muddy boots when suddenly she stopped.

What was that on the table? A fat manila packet, still damp. In her own handwriting it said, Friedrich Bhaer, 11 Waverly Place. Jo seized the envelope and opened it. Inside she discovered a bound book. The title page said, A novel by Josephine March. James T. Fields, Publishers, New York.

She flipped through the pages. Her hands trembled. "Hannah!" she shouted excitedly. "It's my book! Someone has published my book!"

"Heaven take us!" Hannah said when she came into the kitchen, wiping her hands on her apron.

Jo shook the envelope. "There's no letter. How did it get here?"

"Foreign gentleman brung it. Strange kind of name. Can't think of it," Hannah said, carefully examining the pages. "Fox or Bear or such."

"Bhaer?"

"Seemed more of a gentleman than a delivery boy."

"Did you ask him to wait?" Jo asked desperately. "Where did he go?"

"He said he couldn't stay. Said he had a train to catch."

Without pausing to grab an umbrella, Jo burst out of the back door into the rain. She looked up and down the street but could not see the professor anywhere. She raced up the road toward the train station, sloshing through puddles. Still no professor. What if she had missed him altogether?

"Friedrich!" she shouted when she saw a familiar lumbering shape disappearing down Main Street. He held a carpetbag in one hand, an umbrella in the other. She ran to him, filled with sudden happiness. "Thank you for my book!"

His face lit up as if he were delighted to see her, too. "Reading it was like opening a window and looking into your heart," he said.

"When I didn't hear from you, I thought you hated it."

"No, no! It's just that I've been away many places lecturing." He motioned for Jo to join him under the big umbrella. "After you left New York, I made myself very busy. But when I came back and found your wonderful manuscript, I had to show it to Fields. I could not keep such a book to myself."

Jo smiled shyly. She adjusted her soggy bonnet and glanced self-consciously at her muddy skirt and her boots, which were splashed to the ankles. "Friedrich, I can't thank you enough."

"I did nothing. James Fields took it out of my hands and wouldn't give it back. I thought, Such news I should tell her myself."

"I'm happy you did," Jo said, and took his arm. "Please come and meet my family. They have heard so much about you already."

The professor would not budge. "Please apologize to them but I have only a short time between trains. I am on my way back to New York."

"To lecture?"

"No, I am going west to San Francisco. The Union Pacific leaves tomorrow morning."

"You're going to California?" Jo said, stunned.

"The schools are young there. They don't mind a different way of teaching. And I fear there is nothing to keep me here."

Jo gulped. It seemed to her as if her heart had stopped. She could think of nothing to say, nothing to do.

The professor took her hand very formally. "So we will say goodbye."

"It—it was kind of you to bring me news of my book," she stammered. She watched him walk away.

He stopped and at the last moment turned awkwardly to her again. "It was selfish. I thought perhaps she will say, 'Friedrich, don't go so far away.' Though I know that you could never need me as I have needed you."

Jo ran to him, radiant with happiness. "That

isn't true! I have never wanted to be with anyone as I want to be with you."

The professor paused and lowered the umbrella, as if he did not notice the drizzle anymore. He studied Jo's face intently.

"Please don't go so far away," Jo pleaded. "Say you'll stay here and let us make a wonderful life together. We'll do something splendid, something that will turn the world upside down."

The professor smiled. "I will, of course I will. But I have nothing to give you. My hands are empty."

Jo tenderly placed her hands in his. "Not empty now."

The professor lifted the battered umbrella and kissed Jo. Together they walked arm in arm through the rain, mud, and darkness toward the three-story brown clapboard house on the corner of Hawthorne and Lexington roads. Jo unlatched the gate and showed him the way up the walk, closer and closer to the light and warmth of her family's house. With a glad "Welcome home!" she opened the door and led him inside.

LAURIE LAWLOR

Trained as a journalist, Laurie Lawlor worked for many years as a freelance writer and editor before devoting herself full-time to the creation of children's books. She enjoys many speaking engagements at schools and libraries, and her books have been nominated for many awards. She lives in Evanston, Illinois, with her husband, son, daughter, and two large Labrador retrievers. Her books include *Addie Across the Prairie, Addie's Dakota Winter, How to Survive Third Grade,* and *The Worm Club.*

LOUISA MAY ALCOTT

Born in 1832, Louisa May Alcott was the second child of Bronson Alcott of Concord, Massachusetts, a self-taught philosopher and social reformer. Even as a young woman, Louisa May helped support her family. She taught school, worked as a seamstress and nurse, and hired herself out as a domestic servant. At age twenty-one she began publishing poems and sketches. She first achieved financial success writing thrillers under the pen name A. M. Barnard. She became famous under her own name in 1868, when *Little Women* was published. The book was based on her own childhood experiences. In it Alcott depicted herself as Jo and re-created the lively spirits of her three sisters in Meg, Beth, and Amy. She continued the story begun in *Little Women* in *Little Men* (1871) and *Jo's Boys* (1886). Louisa May Alcott died in Boston, in March 1888.

An all-new series of novels based on your
favorite character from the hit TV series!

FULL HOUSE™
Stephanie

Phone Call From a Flamingo
The Boy-Oh-Boy Next Door
Twin Troubles
Hip Hop Till You Drop
Here Comes the Brand-New Me
The Secret's Out

LOOK FOR THESE NEW ADVENTURES
COMING IN 1995:
DADDY'S NOT-SO-LITTLE GIRL
(available mid-December)
P.S. FRIENDS FOREVER
(available mid-January)

Available from Minstrel® Books
Published by Pocket Books